also by Sandra Shwayder Sanchez

The Nun, a novel

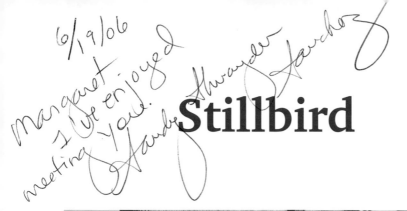

6/19/06
Margaret,
I too enjoyed
meeting you.
Sandy Shwayder Sanchez

Stillbird

a novel
by

Sandra Shwayder Sanchez

The Wessex Collective, 2005

Stillbird © 2005 by Sandra Shwayder Sanchez

ISBN 0-9766274-1-8

Published by   The Wessex Collective
                1955 Holly
                Denver, CO 80220

Web: http://www.wessexcollective.com
contact: sss@wessexcollective.com

Cover drawing by Jeanne Hershorn

Printed by Thomson-Shore, Inc., Dexter MI

The Wessex Collective, publisher of progressive books:

If literary fiction (story telling) is the way that human beings can understand and describe what history feels like, we believe it should be relevant
to universal and historic human experience. We believe also that literary
fiction provides an opportunity to recognize, with significant impact, the
problems of societies as well as individuals. At The Wessex Collective we
are publishing books that demonstrate an empathy for human vulnerability
and an understanding of how that is important to the larger society.

Contents

Dedicated to the Angelas who every day overcome hardships in order to know joy

Part I

Stillbird

I.

"I am lakes trapped in granite caverns
and moss that shrouds the stone..."

Rosie dutifully threw the first clod of grey and sour soil into Jamie's shallow grave. Jamie's last dying words to his brother had been not to waste the fertile bottomland on his grave. Bottomland was meant for living things. And then he had slowly and carefully directed Abel to the spot where he desired to be buried. Abel easily located the spot his brother described near an ancient oak tree that had long ago fallen but lived on, held in place by a large boulder that broke the tree's fall, and that boulder would be Jamie's tombstone.

Abel was bitter, for it was the spot where they had both first seen Rosie, as gloriously beautiful as the red and golden leaves that drifted from the oak and maple trees, covering the landscape in magic. But Abel set about his task and grimly coaxed a grave from the western West Virginia bedrock. It was an act of love that Rosie would never understand.

Then Abel shoveled in the rest, the soil and small rocks and leaves, for it was autumn again, only the second to pass since Rosie fell in love with Jamie and left her own people to marry him. She took the name he gave her and abandoned the one her own mother had bestowed upon her so carefully and ceremonially. Rosie had put herself among the frightening, albeit occasional, company of white men for love of Jamie. She felt her only safety was their respect for his love of her, and now he was dead and she had no one to protect her. Rosie thought all this with urgency while her body stood impassive by the grave and she poised herself for flight, never letting the slightest movement, the briefest expression in her eyes betray this preparation. Even as she longed to hear her Indian name again, she answered to Rosie.

She had thought, as Jamie lay dying of the fever, that he was abandoning her and she should leave then and save herself. But he kept calling that name that wasn't really hers but still belonged to their love as long as they were together, and she did love him still and couldn't bring herself to let him call that name in silence. She sang to him until long after he was stilled and took comfort in the fact that her music eased his pain. He told her this and she knew it was true. He called for his brother and she dreaded going after Abel alone, but Abel came without her summons, as if he'd been listening, and the two men whispered briefly and then Abel went off to dig the grave while Jamie held Rosie's hand and finished his dying.

Remembering, Rosie realized she could not have left any sooner and she wondered how much longer it would be before Abel would leave her alone so she could change into Jamie's clothes and make her way, unhampered by skirts, through the night woods to search for her people. Rosie's people had learned the ways of secrecy early on when they had been herded like cattle across many lands to the west. A few had managed to hide from the United States soldiers and never joined the forced march into exile, and these had lived like ghosts in the wooded hills, moving about like rumors.

But Abel would not leave her alone, worrying about her, loving her as he had always loved her from the first moment he saw her, a vision in the dusky autumn light. Abel would stay to protect her and keep her as his own. He remembered with unfathomable bitterness that when his own mother had been abandoned, no one had stepped forth to claim her as a bride, a married woman in the community. There had been no brothers to undertake this duty for his father and none of the unmarried men of their village had courted her either. And so she had been forced into working as a midwife, bringing other women's children into the world and risking the fear and contempt of the village, dying finally mysteriously and leaving her two sons to their own uncertain destiny, exiled from their home…exiled…alone…Abel remembered and tried to put it behind him, not wishing to dwell on a past he could not change. Oh but that past had haunted him every waking and sleeping moment if he'd but paid attention. Now he thought only to protect Rosie. He truly did love her.

✢

Alwyn was a midwife in the village of Dunvegan on the isle of Skye. On December 24, 1880, she was called to the bedside of young Margaret Macfarland. It was Margaret's first child and the girl barely showed her pregnancy, but still her husband had waited too long to get help, and Alwyn knew when she reached up inside the girl that the child was already dead. The baby, a boy, so all the more to be mourned, was turned backside down and seemed to have the cord wrapped around his neck. Alwyn had to cut him out of the mother to save her if it wasn't too late, but the husband protested, not understanding or believing his son was dead and his wife soon would be. Alwyn gave him something to drink to calm him and reassured him she had done this before and that it was necessary to save his beloved wife's life, but even so, the young Margaret died in this useless begetting, and the man, crazed, would have killed Alwyn then and there had he not been distracted by the cry of an owl and then dazed with grief.

Stillborn babes and mothers who died in childbed were not unheard of in the village, but this terrible event happened on Christmas Eve, and the husband had no other children or family to comfort him, he and Margaret being both orphans. No one grieved more for him than Alwyn herself, but there was nothing she could say, and certainly he would not have listened. That Christmas was a time for mourning and the entire village forgot to celebrate the other birth that was meant to give them joy even in the midst of just such troubles as these. And it was cold, colder than any Christmas that anyone, even the elders, could remember in the history of the village, and such a poor time, no one having quite enough to eat. Even those that barely knew the girl were ready to believe the husband that Alwyn was a witch and had done this thing for her own purposes. And even those who professed not to believe in witches and fairies couldn't deny that there was the sound of human grief in the timbre of the wind in the woods at night, a constant crying that haunted the season.

Abel and James, Alwyn's two sons, heard the odd whisper here, saw the furtive glance there, and they made plans to take their mother to the new world, coaxing work from reluctant villagers to earn their passage. They did not want to stay where they were shunned; they never dreamed the full extent of their danger.

The night of the spring solstice there was music everywhere and even the gods could not have sorted out the strands of supplication, despair or joyous delusion in the frenzied chorus. Alwyn's voice surely joined the singing during the night, but by morning her voice was stilled, her strangled body already a part of the petrification of wood and stone and soil that throbbed a slow eternal life hidden in the mist.

In the mist they buried her, the two boys, now men, before her body could be found and burned as a witch, and they left no marker but marked the spot in their own hearts by the scent of the place, the smell and sound of running water not far off, and the shape of the light through the trees. Then they went to the river to drink, to pray and to love her fully before turning their minds to the sea voyage ahead of them. Each gathered his own memories to last a lifetime. Abel longed to keep her eyes, the deep, dark, loving eyes a mother turns on her first born, if ever so briefly. James struggled to resurrect the scent of her, a scent of herbs and earth. Each would find her alive and real beneath an old oak that lived half uprooted on the strength of a flat-topped boulder at the other side of the world, but she would choose James.

✣

Abel sat in the rocker that Jamie had made for Rosie as a wedding gift and rocked slowly back and forth, saying nothing, forming the words in his mind, discarding them, re-forming them, until he stopped trying to figure out how to talk to Rosie and allowed himself to be lost in memories and fantasies.

Rosie sat on the straight back chair behind the supper table and watched him. Once she asked if he would be wanting some supper. She had rabbit stew and began to build the fire in the cookstove, but Abel only muttered that he was not hungry, and she realized that she wasn't either. Nonetheless, she lit the fire as the sun was setting, and a chill came over them. She lit the lamp at the head of the table where Jamie last sat and left her own face in shadow. She sat back down and watched Abel, not talking.

As the sun sank lower behind the mountain west of the house, a boy came toward them on a pony, a sturdy mountain pony plodding up the steep hillside from the south. Rosie went out on the porch to watch his progress and to once again watch the dusk embrace the trees and the river. She had missed this time of day, the most beautiful after the dawn, when the mists lifted to reveal the landscape. She had been holding Jamie's hand in the constant dusk of the upstairs bedroom, nothing more than a loft really, with a quilt hung over the one window because the light hurt his feverish eyes, or perhaps because he couldn't bear to see the mountain that he was leaving.

Now she let herself be carried into the mystery of the evening, listened for the birds in the forest and watched the boy approach as if she were alone. Abel had followed her out but said nothing, waiting for the strange visit to be over.

The boy, named Peter, brought food: bread made with honey, apples, onions cooked in butter until they were sweet; all this from his mother who was also a new widow, who remembered that when her man had died that summer, it had been Jamie who helped her get her hay in, and now she wanted to help his widow. Peter was to tell her what Rosie needed. Peter recognized Abel, and they spoke briefly. Then Rosie thanked him and he promised to come by soon again, but Abel told him that would not be necessary, and they watched Peter's pony plod back down the mountain. Then Abel found the words to tell Rosie he would protect her.

By now the sun had completed its disappearance and the moon had begun its ascent, lighting Abel's large, powerful figure. Rosie knew better than to reject him outright and told him only that her mind and soul were still with Jamie in the grave and she could hardly think. She asked for time to sleep, and Abel went silently down the mountain after Peter, leaving her to grieve. But Abel had nowhere he wanted to go and walked only as far as his brother's grave, not to remember his brother, but to remember the first time he had seen Rosie and to wait for her there.

There was a sheltered spot between the trunk of the oak and the rock where a man could wedge himself and escape the wind, and there Abel sat still watching the moon and waiting for the dawn. He expected Rosie by the dawn, but even her light and quiet footsteps on the autumn leaves near midnight woke him, and he accosted her there at the site of her dead husband's grave.

Abel had never been a man to squander his virility on a woman he didn't want for the mere pleasure of it. His was the passion of a man who had saved himself in every way for this woman. He would make her understand later that this rape was a gift to be cherished, and he was convinced that he would give her a son and then she would love him. He could not charm her with words and eyes that easily expressed his love. His love was deep inside him in a dark place, and he knew no other way to win her than to force her, and he was desperate to win her. If she disappeared back into the forest, she'd be no more than a magical vision he'd never be able to hold onto. This was the only way.

Abel hurt her more, the more she struggled, and Rosie finally stopped fighting him and waited for this invasion to be over. She prayed that he would fall deeply asleep, and long enough for her to escape. As soon as she was certain that his deep and even breathing was not a trick, she rolled quietly away, then crawled down the hill until she was sure that he could no longer see her beneath the scrub and brush. The moon still lit the night, and she prayed for mist and rain to hide her, and slowly, wisps of clouds gathered over the moon, and soon there was a drizzle.

By the time the sun had risen high enough in the sky to burn off the morning mist, Rosie was nowhere to be seen. Abel was sluggish, had slept through the light rain of the night, but he was startled awake by the urgent call of a crow that dipped its wing close to his head and then soared off out of sight. Hundreds of tiny blackbirds that slept in the branches of the old oak tree fluttered awake at the same moment and flew as one, lifting off effortlessly, as if thrown into the air by the invisible hand of the wind, and then settled silently back down into another tree farther up the hillside to bask in the warmth of the mid-morning sun. Geese flew in arrow formation high overhead, and Abel watched them as far as he could see and waited for their barking and screeching to quiet down, so he could listen for Rosie's footsteps. But he could hear nothing after the frenzied morning noises of the birds.

After a while, Abel detected the whisper of a small creek running down the hill and went there to wash, wishing Rosie would be there. He imagined her, a vision of water, transparent and shimmering, her hair floating out around her, a rainbow to his storm. As he walked, disturbing the autumn leaves that rustled and drifted beneath his heavy feet, he remembered watching Rosie and Jamie lying beneath the oak tree that last summer. Jamie lay on a blanket asleep and Rosie, with the hem of her long, full skirt in her hand to make a sack, collected petals of wildflowers all over the hillside and then she stood over Jamie and let her skirt fall, and all the petals of wild roses and laurel blossoms fell, burying Jamie in softness and scent. And then she dropped to her knees as Jamie sat up to embrace her, and they made love, and Abel knew that he should look away, but he never could take his eyes off Rosie. Rosie herself never could look at Abel, looking always past him or down; and she never addressed him by his name, and flinched ever so slightly when he said hers.

Rosie had been born to a mother who had lived her entire life in hiding, and Rosie was brought up to live in hiding. Secrecy saved them from the trail of tears where thousands died en route to the barren lands of the west and secrecy saved them over the years while they acquired land through a white trader who was allowed, as they were not, to purchase it. Secrecy and a will to hold on tightly to one another and the traditional ways saved them from extinction. Knowing this, Rosie knew also that her defection for love of a white man would be viewed as treachery, and she did not expect a warm welcome home over the mountains to North Carolina. She would approach the elders with humility and had already given herself the name "No-name," discarding Jamie's name for her even as she had discarded her parents' name for her when she married him. She knew she would have to earn a new name and the new name would come to her when the time was right. Now, as she crossed from one life to another, she was an empty vessel, waiting for the gift of soul and identity. It was a two-day walk up and over hills following the crow, and she sang most of the way so the days passed quickly. Joy and anxiety mingled and made her heart beat far too fast and hard when she sighted cabins and the smoke of fragrant fires. She fainted there in the woods at the edge of the village and was found like that: near death, it seemed to the women who exclaimed over her.

There was no question of abandoning No-Name, but her return had created a moral dilemma that was resolved by requiring that she continue the exile she herself had chosen when she married Jamie. There was a cabin by the river a day's walk from the village that had been abandoned by white settlers, and No-Name was escorted there and given supplies she would need for her survival. Three of the oldest women of the tribe promised to visit her in a month to see how she was doing, but No-Name knew that she would be watched over from a distance, deprived of company but not of sustenance, and she looked forward with relief to her month of solitude.

In the cabin some things had been left behind: kerosene lamps and some books on a table, two chairs and a bed, almost as if someone had been expected.

No-Name looked at the books, remembering how Jamie had enjoyed teaching her to read. She sounded out the English words, taking no meaning from them, but the memory of Jamie's voice breaking the words into separate syllables so they might have been any language, and it occurred to No-Name that rhythm was the secret of language as it was the secret of music, a subtle trick of transformation. Then she went out to watch the sunlight fade over the river and listen to the evening birds. It was such a lovely starlit night that she decided she wanted to sleep right there by the river with its song loud in her head and she dragged the feather mattress outside and lay it over a bed of leaves that she pushed together. She nestled into the leaves and slept soundly without dreaming, but sometimes she awoke and watched the stars, and when she woke, it seemed the birds did too, and they spoke to her, and she got her name that night: Stillbird-by-the-River was how she would call herself in her heart.

The next day, Stillbird built a fire outside her cabin and boiled river water in a large kettle the old women had given her so she could cook some beans. While the beans simmered in the pot, she walked along the river, stopping to examine everything and listening carefully. She thought she heard voices back by the cabin, whispers that carried on the clear air, and she recognized the women. And when she returned to the cabin, she found an iron stove there and wondered how they had carried such a heavy thing all that way. Then other things began to appear at the cabin that only men could have brought, but she neither saw nor heard a man even when she hid in the woods and spied on the cabin at random times of the day. Jamie had told her that in Scotland the people told stories of fairies that lived in the woods, but he didn't believe in them. And she knew they didn't live here, or she would have heard the same stories. The stories she had heard from her mother were stories about animals and birds and even the river itself, but none of these had been known to cause a sack of flour as heavy as a man to be wafted into a woman's home, nor did they carry things made of iron by the hand of man. Stillbird knew that it was human beings who tricked her so kindly.

The days grew shorter and shorter, but as long as Stillbird could see the gleam of the river in the night, she was not afraid of the darkness. Some nights when she slept, she saw the darkness in Abel's eyes and awoke afraid and looked around to see where she was, and had to work to remember everything that had happened since the rape, to know that she was safe now in the solitude of the woods. She had not told the women about the rape, believing that they would blame her all the more for leaving them in the first place.

As the month drew to an end and Stillbird expected the elders to visit her, she began to burn the books with the English words, page by page, reading them as she tore them out and remembering Jamie, and then forgetting him, for she had crossed over into another life and was waiting to see what would happen to her.

⁜

Every night Abel went to the rock and waited, and sometimes he would call out Rosie's name and then he would listen carefully when he'd flushed a deer or a wild turkey with his crying, and he'd hope until dawn came and showed him the emptiness of the woods; even the crows and the blackbirds had gone, and he could hope no more until lured back by the mysterious darkness of another night.

Abel abandoned his home, taking nothing with him, and lived in the woods, eating wild things that he caught in traps and wandering the paths made by deer. He traveled farther and farther, following the river and visioning women in the stones that sparkled beneath the rushing sunlit water and the clouds that drifted across the stars at night. His mother, he saw just shy of clarity and Rosie, as if she stood right in front of him, so clear he could imagine her chest rise and fall with each breath, and hearing his own deep breath, he would mistake it for hers and call her name softly, but hearing his own voice loud in his head. And then one night when the moon was full again, he saw her sitting by the river. He watched her lit by the gleam of the moonlit water in the night as she stood and wrapped a shawl around her shoulders and walked to a cabin. He did not see the cabin or where she had disappeared to until she lit the lamp inside, and he could watch her through the window as she built a fire and ate something for supper and went to sleep. He wondered at this and couldn't tell if she was alone or not, and so he waited for the day.

⁜

The three elder women of the tribe approached Stillbird's cabin at dawn, quietly until one of them muttered that something was wrong, someone was there, and they all looked around carefully but saw no one and continued on to the cabin to wake Stillbird. They led a pony with a sled on which were the makings of a sweat lodge, and they explained to Stillbird, whom they still called No-Name, that they had come to help her purify herself and to find a new name. They said this was important now, albeit sooner than they would have done, because a young man of the tribe had fallen in love with her and wanted her as his wife. Stillbird realized that he must have brought the stove and the food supplies and she was grateful, but also resentful that he had seen her and she had not seen him, and perhaps they thought she would be so grateful for a husband that she didn't have to look him over first. Stillbird agreed to the ritual of the sweat, but told them she already had a name given to her by the birds of the river, and she told them what it was, and they simply nodded, neither approving nor disapproving, which was the best she was going to get from them, clear enough.

First they laid the boughs in the appropriate ways with the appropriate prayers, and then they covered them with the skins they had brought. They built a fire and heated rocks, and when the rocks were hot enough, they moved them with tongs into the center of the sweat lodge. Then they filled a pot with river water and placed it next to the hot rocks and filed in to huddle close around the rocks.

The sweat had been constructed to accommodate only the four of them and they were crowded over the steaming rocks in the center. The leader started to chant and one by one the others joined her, Stillbird joining in last. As the leader sprinkled river water over the rocks, making more and more steam, Stillbird thought she would faint from the closeness and the extreme heat. She knew she was being tested as well as purified and she never faltered in the chanting, but she put her two hands behind her back and crept her fingers out under the skins to touch the cool earth outside and breathed in the coolness of the earth and a bit of snow through her fingers, and she felt better and stronger. Each time the heat seemed about to overwhelm her, she would reach about with her fingers to find a piece of cold snow and feel it move up through her veins to her shoulders, and thence to her throat and her chest and her head, and she chanted on with the elder women until finally it was over and they all smiled at her as they filed out of the sweat to sit around the fire, catching the smoke and fanning it about their bodies in the continuing ritual of purification.

Hidden in the woods across the river, a young Cherokee man watched, and Abel, hidden in the woods of the hillside above the cabin, watched the man watching the women. Abel went away then thinking to die, then thinking to wait, then waiting to die, and then, when he didn't die, thinking to pray. Abel prayed to women: to Mary mother of God, and Mary Queen of Scotland, and to his mother. And he prayed that he had given Rosie a child, and that she would have no choice but to love him.

II

A woman's voice, neither old nor young, clear as a starry night, sings loud, rough notes into the cold air. Then a man answers and there is the sound of a drum: firm, regular, inexorable drum beats, no grace, no passion, just firm... regular...inexorable. Other men's voices join in before they build to an angry crescendo and abruptly stop. Then another woman's voice, farther away, weak and sad like a sob, and then silence. Silence until dawn, and then the drums again, and bagpipes very loud, almost joyous.

Every night Abel sat with his son by the evening fire and dreamed of the music of his youth and woke up wondering, as he wondered every night, if he would find the woman the next morning.

✧

Sounds resonated off the myriad walls of the cave and Stillbird's imagination formed an eerie music from them. She stared into the fire that burned incessantly, giving her the light and warmth she needed, the gift of the doe killed by the bobcat at the mouth of her cave. She had heard the chase through the woods above the cave, and then the doe had stood absolutely still at the entrance of Stillbird's home and their eyes met. The doe waited there for the cat and had given her life then for Stillbird. After the cat had eaten all she could of the meat and fed her young cubs, she fended off the wild dogs so Stillbird could eat as well. After Stillbird had taken chunks of meat inside her cave to cook, the vultures came and cleaned the bones. Stillbird brought the bones deep inside the cave, into the second room that could not be seen from outside, and lit her fire of bones and wood she had gathered by moonlight. The doe's bones burned long and hot and lasted until Stillbird found other older bones, skulls and hip bones, bones that were caught in flight and bones that still smelled of fear. Sometimes the big cat dragged her prey to the mouth of the cave and ate there in Stillbird's presence, leaving some meat and the bones behind.

Once Abel felled a doe with his arrow and tracked the carcass to the cave. He would have found Stillbird then, but the cat ran down from the hill above and frightened him away.

Stillbird listened to ancient, magical music and watched the flames, remembering the events of the past fifteen winters that led up to her living in this cave with animal guardians, entrusting her life and death to the earth that hid and nurtured her.

⁜

After the second sweat, Stillbird felt dizzy and faint, and the three women had to catch and hold her as she struggled to reach the bank of the river, and they helped lay her down there to rest.

When she was strong enough to sit and walk, the woman who had stayed to watch over her whispered in a distant way, "we'll do this one more time after your moon and then you will be ready to marry," and Stillbird told her she had not bled for two moons now, and she told her about the rape, in a distant voice, as if neither woman was even there, as if this were happening to someone else in another place and time, in a tale perhaps, and she was waiting to hear the end. The older woman said nothing for a long time, then only, "we'll see," and then she left quietly while Stillbird paid attention to other voices inside herself, voices that told her there would be no marriage, she would remain alone, give birth alone. She tried to calm herself, tried to be not afraid, and soon she was calm and not afraid. She did not notice the old woman leave, for she was so used to her solitude.

All through the winter Stillbird worked hard to keep warm, getting up early enough to watch the dawn and give herself spiritual strength for the day and then walking miles gathering wood that was dry enough and small enough for her fire. She had made a sled from the sweat lodge skins and poles that the women left behind, and well it was blessed, her sled, for on it she carried fuel to survive an unusually harsh winter. Sometimes she thought she heard footsteps and would stand still listening, not admitting that she hoped it was the mysterious young man who had once wanted to make her his wife. She only thought that on the coldest days, or days when her bones ached, and she felt old before her years, in need of some human warmth, some soft human voice to say nothing in particular, just make a soothing sound, the feel of warm, strong arms around her chilled and aching body when the night should have been over long ago, but lasted longer and longer, damper and colder, until the solstice brought slightly shorter nights, slightly longer days and within days, the appearance of tiny, tentative buds, if she looked very, very carefully. Then her spirits lifted and she chastised herself for even thinking of marriage. She was fine alone, she preferred her solitude and her freedom. Of course that would all change when the child was born, but that would not happen until mid-summer and she thanked all the gods for that; that her child would have a head start on the cold of another winter. For now she took her life one day at a time, treasuring each exquisite dawn, grateful for the abundance of wood and the deep penetration of the warmth of the fire. It was only during those hours before the dawn, when the fire died and her soul seemed to die with it, despairing in the dark, that she fell prey to fears she felt keenly but could not understand. She prayed to sleep through those hours, and when she couldn't, she prayed to remain calm and be not afraid, to remember that each night those hours passed and left her still alive and well, alone and free, the same from one day to the next.

So, she survived the worst of winter and stopped to see who made the sounds in the forest, hoping not for the sight of the man, but for the sight of a deer. She practiced with the bow and arrows she had found on her front porch one day so she could have meat. She also, often, found wood. At first these gifts had given her the hope, the idea, that her suitor was still courting, but once she saw the three women bringing the wood on their sled and she knew that the elders were looking after her, even though there was no longer any intention of bringing her back within the society of her people anytime soon. Perhaps never, and if ever, it would remain to be seen after her baby was born. Perhaps they would wait for a sign and the sign would come with the child or through the child. This Stillbird knew and accepted.

Though she had never seen his face, and never known him at all, Stillbird felt a vague resentment for the young man who dared to love her without knowing her and dared to discard her when he learned just one thing about her, as if her worth as a woman was measured by her victimization by another man. And she wondered if this high and mighty suitor would have done the same deed, the rape; if he perhaps had not raped some other woman, some other place and time. She caught herself hating a man she could not visualize and thinking less of Abel, whom she hated to visualize. His face in her mind made her afraid and she fought the urge to forgive, to feel sorry for him, and reminded herself that no man, not Abel, not the young unknown, unseen suitor, not even Jamie would have felt sorry for her in her grief. She was better off with the mist and the dawn in the morning, the woods during the day and the moon and stars at night, the sound of rain on her roof, the cry of the owl that nested close by, the footfalls of the deer that occasionally showed themselves and, less often, sacrificed themselves for her to eat. She became a good hunter and gatherer. When spring came and the elders left seeds and tools at her door, another hint that she was expected to continue fending for herself, she set to work to clear a garden.

As Stillbird vigorously broke ground she recalled early days of childhood when she had loved her father and felt so proud to see the way he looked at her beautiful mother. They were so loving and tender together, just the three of them, and her father never hinted in any way that he was not thoroughly pleased with her. But then her mother had the first of three miscarriages, late enough along in the pregnancy that her father could see it was a boy they had lost, and he seemed to grieve as much over that fact as he did over losing their child. It was brief and subtle, but even at the age of four, she felt a pang so sharp she remembered it vividly and with a keen anger even now, twenty years later. Her father treated her mother then even more tenderly, comforting her for her loss, and this seemed appropriate for a while, but after several weeks, she wanted to shout at them and remind them that they still had her, and it hurt that she had to remind them of the joy they used to feel when they watched her play. Perhaps she was expected to be a grown-up already, someone to be relied upon to care for younger children. She became more thoughtful then, did not often smile, and then, after neglecting her in their grief, they had the gall to chide her for not being cheerful.

After the second miscarriage her father grew distant, and after the third, he hardly paid attention to either his wife or his daughter, except when he was irritated with them for some silly little thing. Then her mother died in her last attempt to give her husband a son, and if Stillbird remembered being angry before that time, she had to sit down and cry right there in the garden over the hurt and anger she felt when her father remarried a young woman not four full moons after her own mother was gone. She was twelve then and finally a woman herself, and fully aware of her father's selfishness, and she vowed she would never marry a man so careless of her feelings and her person. Her father had been young and sweet once, she remembered it, and that memory made her suspicious of the young men who courted her so sweetly.

What drew her to Jamie was his difference, plain and simple. He was so foreign she trusted him to be somehow better than the men she compared to her father. And then he said to her one day that he wanted to care for her and her alone forever; didn't want children…she made him repeat it because she never heard of a man that didn't want a little replica of himself, and he explained that she would be his child, so of course she said yes, she would marry him, and it had delighted her that her father felt the hurt and the anger that she had lived with all those years. She could see it in his eyes that he felt her choice to be a rejection of himself, and she gloried in her revenge until he died a year later and she realized the pettiness of revenge in the face of the irrevocability of death. But there was that woman and her two sons to mourn him, and she felt a kind of sad wisdom more than grief when they brought her the news. And it was the sad part of wisdom that hit her when Jamie lay dying of the same disease that took her father, and she realized that it was Jamie who had been the child and wanted no competition for her attention. She didn't blame him. She knew he had believed what he told her when he said it and probably believed it until he closed his eyes, his hand in hers, that last forever time.

So Stillbird sat in the garden, grasping a handful of earth in her hands, wringing her hands, holding herself and burying her face in her skirt, crying and crying, loudly, vigorously, until she was tired and then she put it away, tired enough to sleep well that night.

Abel wanted to run and comfort her but he knew he had to wait until the baby was born. He followed her life with confidence now that the other man was out of it, and even the three old women came seldom to Stillbird's cabin, and then, only when she was away. Abel didn't understand them, but her isolation suited him fine, and he spent his nights thinking of all the kind things he would do for her and how grateful to him she would be, how loving and grateful.

✣

Abel laughed and laughed as the geese skidded onto the lake making large noisy splashes, rainbow waves in the sun. He sat high on his father's shoulders and could look up at the bellies of the birds as they arrowed in for their spectacular water landings, barking and screeching with prideful challenge and delight. The geese were not afraid of them. Abel's father brought him often to the spot to watch the geese, but after Jamie was born everything changed. Abel remembered the spot by the lake as the scene of his happiest memories.

Later when he was a grown man but still a child inside his heart, he followed his mother to that selfsame spot and watched her sit and stare at the birds. Finally he revealed himself and sat next to her and spoke to her. Abel told his mother all about the happiest moment of his life, the last time his father brought him to the lake to laugh at the geese and he laughed to remember it, until he realized that Alwyn was not listening, had not heard a word, did not care. And Abel knew that she was thinking of other different scenes, remembering how the man beat them after Jamie was born. Abel never understood why and knew better than to ask his mother. She couldn't explain it. She was simply glad when the man left.

Year after year she avoided suitors as drunk and foolish and cruel as her husband had been by invoking his name and the belief that he would return, and she didn't mind that they laughed at her. Better that derision than resentment, she thought, and would have been right, but in time the derision turned into resentment when it finally dawned on them, the bachelors of the village, that it was the woman who was laughing at them. And then weren't they only too glad to believe that she had worked some evil spell on young Margaret MacFarland, depriving her husband not only of that child but a good wife and more children to come? Hadn't she been heard to say that men didn't know any better but to beat the women and children they professed to love and want so much? One brief but unforgettable moment of angry truth telling that would haunt them until her death; be the death of her in fact. And did her sons understand any of it? All Abel knew was that Alwyn hid Jamie in a cupboard when his father came home, and he, the older child, had to hide himself. And then those times his father found him, he made it clear enough he was angry, because his own beloved son was hiding from him, and wasn't it his mother who told him to do it? Able didn't understand that anything would have infuriated his father, that his father was already infuriated before he took even the first shot of whiskey. Abel never understood it and neither did Alwyn. She tried to tell Abel it was not his fault. He was so sad when his father left. He'd been thinking that the anger would subside and that one day he and his father would go once again to the lake to laugh at the geese, and he never really lost hope of that until his father went away for days, then months, then years, and his mother was glad. Abel blamed her for that so they could not speak of it, and not speaking of what they thought the most about, they could not speak of anything else either.

Alwyn talked of many things with Jamie but Abel never inquired as to their conversations, being proud and feeling left out. And yet he loved her and when she died her terrible, mysterious death, he missed her more than he had ever missed his father. He was upset with himself but didn't know why. He didn't reproach himself for failing to tell his mother he loved her, because he never knew he was supposed to do that. Her death was so sudden, and then they were gone to another world, and the old world seemed to have sunk into the sea with the father, the mother, the laughter, and all the love he could vaguely remember. Until he saw Rosie the first time and dreamt that he was looking up at the bellies of noisy geese who splashed down into a lake of rainbows and reflections so beautiful that he woke himself up with his own choked cries. All Abel knew of life was loss.

✣

Winter did not want to let go that year and there was one last cold spell and snowstorm after Stillbird had finished her spring planting. Fortunately the seeds were still hidden beneath the earth and wouldn't send up tiny green shoots until the snow was rapidly melting in the sun and its moisture only gave them greater strength. Stillbird enjoyed the crispness of that last snow beneath the brilliant blue sky and walked miles every day sniffing the air and examining everything in her slow, serious way, so focused on the birds that took flight before her step, the buds that gave the trees a lacy look in the morning sunshine. Her pregnancy was finally showing, and she could feel the baby move inside her and sometimes even see her stomach jump here and there, and she laughed to imagine an elbow or knee poking out in some kind of fretful dance. "I want to get out"…"I want to get out," she half screamed, half sang, feeling such a love and kinship for the baby inside her…"and how I want you out where I can see you and touch you," she whispered back again and again, talking now to the one other human being that inhabited her world where she walked in beauty every day and exulted in it every night.

Spring was indeed a wonderful time. Dried out creek beds filled up with rushing streams that came up in the night and surprised Stillbird during her dawn walks. They would be gone again by mid-summer, but for the few weeks that they serenaded her, she would make daily pilgrimages to each spot, deeming it sacred and staying sometimes until dusk, just listening to the music of the water and watching the reflections of leaves and rocks and light on the current. She would put her hand down upon the surface of the moving water, letting it sculpt her hand with its own shapes, changing shapes constantly and quickly, mesmerizing the young mother, soothing the child inside her, she was sure. When the sun was strong and hot, she would undress and bathe in the icy water, feeling thereafter not only cleaner but stronger. She had no idea that Abel followed her on these sacred walks and watched her every move and watched her for hours when she didn't move at all.

He knew before she did when the elders of her people came and left gifts for the coming child, and he knew before she did when soldiers and settlers came and massacred her people, all the men and the women and children, scarcely a hundred of them and then gone, everyone, without a trace but the added richness of the soil where the bodies were buried and the blood and the ash from the burned village seeped into the soil where white farmers would plant their crops until they themselves were overtaken by disaster, seemingly less violent but ultimately as catastrophic: those very farmers and their children run down by a civilization that raped the earth even as men continued to kill each other and rape women. Not even Abel could foresee these things. He felt nothing as he watched the fate of the village unfold, the cries of women reminded him of his mother, but he was too engrossed in what he had to do next…go see her, tell her and offer his protection once again and pray that she would be grateful and love him. He decided to wait until the baby was born. He knew she would be more willing then.

Stillbird was in her garden when the baby began to push out of her, thinning the plants, weeding out the wild things, caressing the earth the way she did as she squatted in the garden. It was squatting in the garden that she gave birth to a little boy and wrapped him in her long skirt to take him to the river to wash off the blood, her own blood, and take a good look at him and show him to the sun and the birds. It was a warm June day, but not too hot, and she and her child were healthy and strong and happy to be together finally. It was a good day, the best day of Stillbird's life, and she would always remember it as if it were yesterday, and sometimes that vivid memory would warm her heart, and sometimes it would make her cry out long and loud in anger and betrayal, but on that day, she was content as the animals of the woods and sang softly to herself and her son. She was so young she thought that beginning was an ending, a happy ending.

The elders had left things for the baby, and Stillbird hoped that they would have observed that her child was born now and come back to see her face to face, with or without gifts, but with words of welcome home, because she knew she did not want to raise her son in isolation. She was ready now to end her solitude and give her son the gift of family and identity. Each day she waited to see them, listening carefully to the sounds she heard in the woods, but each day she heard only the birds, the deer, once a bobcat, once a bear. They came close to the house and watched and she watched them back from her porch, prepared to defend her child but not needing to, as the animals walked quietly away back into the woods.

She never left her cabin those first couple weeks of the baby's life, nursing him whenever he cried, falling asleep with him at her breast, feeling peaceful but with just the edge of anxiety invading her mood as the days passed and the old women did not come for her. They never said they would, but Stillbird understood that they would and expected them, told herself they were testing her patience and tried to be patient and then began to worry again. "Where are they, where are they?" she would ask the infant who looked at her, raised his tiny arm to caress her breast as he nursed, gurgled, fell asleep. Each day Stillbird sang to her son less cheerfully, more fearfully, and softly, so she could hear the footsteps in the woods. And then he came. Abel appeared at her door and Stillbird couldn't move, held her son closer to her breast as if to hide him, stared and kept her fear hidden, stared and waited to hear what the man would say.

III

"I'm sorry, I'm sorry," was all he could say for several minutes, and Stillbird thought he was apologizing to her for the rape and started to tell him it was over long ago and she was okay and to please go away because she did not want to see him there, and she didn't need him. But he kept saying it, and then he said he'd take care of her and that she would not have to be all alone, and finally she asked, "What?"

"They got everyone, even the women and the children and there was nothing anyone could do. They surprised them, and the men weren't ready for them, and anyway, they were outnumbered. The farmers had soldiers with them."

"What are you talking about?"

"You know nothing of this do you? Of course there was no one left to come to you, to tell you, and no warning of what was going to happen until it was too late. The young man who came here sometimes, he was one of the first they killed. The three old women were among the last, but they were killed also. They spared no one, no one. And then they buried them all in a large ditch. All the soldiers dug and the farmers helped, and then they dumped all the bodies in the ditch one on top of the other, unholy it was, and then they burned the cabins…"

And Stillbird simply stared, trying to listen as fast as Abel talked, and Abel talked faster than he ever had, having more to say than he could keep up with. And now he would tell her about the massacre, and now he would tell her he would take care of her, and then back to the terrible story of her people, and then back to the terrible story of his heart.

Stillbird tried to scream but no sound came out, and she wanted to cry but her throat and eyes were dry, and she wanted to move, get away from Abel by the door but her legs wouldn't work, and thank God her arms were paralyzed around her baby, or she would have dropped him, she couldn't even feel him there in her arms, but she remained stuck around him in place, in front of the man who had come finally after all those days of waiting for someone to come and take her away from her loneliness.

She allowed Abel to come closer, to touch her, to walk her to a chair and sit her down and then change his mind and pick her up and carry her and the baby to the bed and lay them down there. And Stillbird fell asleep there with her child in her arms, and she didn't wake again until she felt Abel loosen the front of her dress to let the baby nurse, and she didn't stop him or move to help herself but suffered his touch meekly, almost thankfully, because she still couldn't move or cry or even say the softest word. And so it was for two more days, and Abel was so gentle with her and the baby. He fed her food that he cooked, spoonful by spoonful, as if she were the infant, and he spoke softly to her and cajoled her to eat so she would have milk for the baby, like he knew all about it. He kept telling her how sorry he was about her people, and he seemed to know them, but it was days before it occurred to Stillbird to wonder how he knew them. Her people had refused to meet Jamie or his brother when she married, and she began to think about that and wondered with a terrible dread how Abel knew these people, and then all of his kindness seemed sinister, but she didn't know what to do, and she knew she had to go with him. How long had he been watching her? From the very beginning? She knew she could never hide from him and that he would persist until he found her wherever she could go, and she didn't know anywhere she could go, with her own people dead, massacred by soldiers just like in the stories her mother had told her about the years before the war. It was still happening, and they had thought it was over finally. Stillbird was too tired and too shocked for rage; it was the sad part of wisdom that crept into her soul then and made her quiet and calm as she prepared to follow Abel back to the home he promised her. She had nowhere else to go, not with an infant, his infant at that.

Abel took Stillbird and his son, whom he named Charles after a king of Scotland, back to the cabin that Jamie had built for his wife, thinking that Stillbird would feel more at home there than in the bachelor quarters he had constructed for himself on the land that he and his brother had homesteaded together when they first came to this land. Stillbird didn't care and had no reaction. She thought back in those early days of their life together that she should try to appease him, but she could not find within herself enough feeling to smile at anything, and this hurt him, she could see. She truly did feel sorry for him then, right along with her fear of him. She was confused and tried to be careful, but that carefulness on her part made him feel more desperate to please and then angry, not at her, but at life. They both sought refuge from this intolerable situation by concentrating their attention on the baby, and both were kind to the child and took joy from his innocent radiance and satisfaction from his utter dependence on them.

Their first two years together were peaceful and could have been romantic had Stillbird been inclined to love Abel at all. He courted her each and every day, touching her only with his eyes and tender words that he composed carefully and spoke with a childlike yearning. He brought her all the early spring blossoms and especially those he noticed she preferred when she walked out in the woods. More than the wild roses or exotic azalea blossoms, Stillbird loved lilacs and often broke off a sprig to carry with her throughout the day. Perhaps remembering a scene Stillbird didn't know he had witnessed, Abel filled their bed with lilac blossoms one April night and begged her to let him love her gently, promising he'd never be rough with her again, and because she was tired of his unshed tears, she suffered him to enter her person a second time. Every day thereafter, she drank a cautious measure of tansy tea in order to avert another pregnancy without harming herself. Whether due to the tea or timing, Stillbird did not get pregnant again, not then, not ever, and for that she thanked the creator every morning. In her heart she planned to disappear, to die if necessary, as soon as Charles was grown and had made his own life. She could not envision tolerating Abel for any other reason but her son's safety.

Sometimes she tried to look at Abel differently, to find what was good and beautiful in him, and she would tell herself that he was a kind and loving father and that should count for something, and certainly he treated her with a gentleness she could not fault. But she could not forget the first violence and even his gentleness had an intensity to it that disturbed her, as if she herself were so fragile and precious that he couldn't see her as flesh and blood.

Jamie had compared her to the wildflowers of the woods and named her Rosie. Abel compared her secretly in his heart to some ethereal idea he did not share with her and gave her no name at all, and she left him there, lacking that intimate and powerful connection: knowledge of who she was. He was hurt by this and hurt by her each and every day, as each and every day, he failed to win her love, and couldn't accept that she would never forgive the rape, and forgetting that she had rejected him even before the rape. Speaking only half his thought, he would often say, "But we have Charles." And Stillbird, feeling that sad part of wisdom, would let him hold her hand and she'd respond, "Yes, we have got Charles."

One morning when Charlie was two years old, he toddled out to the front porch and was fascinated to see a long rope-like thing lying in the sunny patch on the weathered boards. Charlie reached out to touch the snake, but Stillbird quietly put one hand over her son's outreached hand and with the other, she gently laid a finger over his lips. She stared into her son's eyes and whispered to him not to disturb the snake and then she showed him how to keep a quiet and respectful distance from the snake while she carried him inside. Later the snake slithered off the porch and Charlie watched from the doorway, fascinated by the sudden sinuous movement. He'd never seen anything so fast. Stillbird explained to Charlie he needed to stay away from snakes and never try to touch one unless she herself told him it was okay. When Abel came home from working the hay field, his son was so excited to tell his father about the snake. Talking was exciting to him, and Abel suspected that Stillbird talked far more to the baby than to her husband, or where would the child find so many words? Abel was angry that Stillbird could talk so freely to the child but said only what she had to to him, and often Abel would hide and listen to her talk and sing to Charlie just to hear the sound of her voice with joy in it. But he realized he was a guilty man and could not blame her for this.

He could blame her, however, for her failure to protect their son. When Charlie was finished telling his story, perhaps before he was quite finished, Abel asked Stillbird in a puzzled voice why she had not taken the shotgun by the door and killed the snake? Before she could respond, he asked her in a voice that was puzzled and harsh why didn't she think the snake would come back? Or didn't she care? Didn't she believe it was a danger to Charlie? Didn't she think at all? Were Indian women so careless of their children? No wonder some folks called Indians savages. Whereupon Stillbird protested, quiet-like and puzzled herself, and Abel slapped her hard across her face and told her never to talk back to him again.

Stillbird was stunned and stood still and staring at Abel full in the face for a long time, for the first time ever, until he had to look away. But he felt victorious. He had confused her and made her look at him, see him; and his power filled him with euphoria. He walked outside, taking the shotgun with him to look for the snake, which he found nested with several others in a pile of rocks by the river. He shot several times, killing a couple of the snakes and stirring up others that slithered into the tall grass like thick, earthy lightening, and then he went back to the house and requested his supper. He was kind but firm with Charlie that night and put him to bed. He made a formal apology to his wife, after which he made love to her, and she was too confused to deny him. He sensed her confusion as fear, which made him first sad and then satisfied: if she would not love him, let her fear him, he would settle for that.

The winters of southern West Virginia were lovely in a soft misty way: the evergreen trees blended with skies of a multitude of soft grays and here and there a splash of some auburn leaves that had clung to the trees despite the wind and occasional snows. And then there were the days of crystal brilliance when snow covered everything in a diamond light that shone beneath perfect blue skies that made Stillbird suck in her breath and want to run. She would walk for miles every day, sometimes letting Abel take Charlie with him to cut the firewood, sometimes taking him with her to search out stray calves grown big enough now to forage on their own. They were lucky to have a strong thermal spring on their property that ran all winter, never froze. And the calves could always drink from its earth-warmed flow. Stillbird would pretend she had to search long and far for this or that calf; she always had a story to tell Abel why she'd been gone so long on those days she left Charlie with him and took only her dreams and her memories for company. Abel understood her preoccupation with the child, but never could understand her preoccupation with solitude. After the incident of the summer she knew she should talk more to Abel, be friendlier to him. But when she brought herself to do this, she noticed that it didn't matter anymore, made things worse because he would snap at her, act as if whatever she said was foolish or flat out wrong. So she went back to her silence and back to her habit of never looking at him. He no longer made love to her, but satisfied his sexual appetite quickly every night with a certain grim dutifulness, as if he had paid good money for her and wanted to be sure he hadn't wasted it. Often when he was done, she would wait until she was certain he was sound asleep and then she would dress and go out to walk in the moonlight cleansing her soul of her shame.

At first only rain or snow could keep Stillbird from her nightly walks and later, not even that. She would spend longer and longer walking the hills in the moonlight, or by the light of stars or backlit clouds, often feeling her way down familiar paths in absolute darkness. When she was overcome with sleepiness she would turn back, and one night she had gone so far that she could not keep on walking home but had to curl up at the root of a large tree to sleep. She awakened at dawn to see a man standing with his back to her and facing the sun lighting up the sky over the mountain. As she watched, she determined that he was painting on a canvas that he had set up on a portable easel. In one hand he held a palette with a space for his thumb and splotched with many colors of paint and with the other, he dabbed at the paint and then the canvas. She stood up very quietly and gently, slowly walked toward him, as if she thought he were an animal that would run if he caught her scent or any sudden movement. Stillbird was so surprised to see another human being, a stranger there, that she wasn't sure he was real, and when he turned and saw her, he also thought he was having a vision. He stared at Stillbird and she stared first at him and then at the painting, which seemed nothing more than a blur of dots of colors. He gestured to her to come closer to examine the painting, and she approached him still warily. Then he spoke and his voice was mild and sweet, low and soft, as if he did not want to disturb the quiet of the dawn, which concluded itself above them in a brilliant rose and then disappeared into an innocent blank sky. The moment of magic was gone and Stillbird was certain that the man was real, his voice louder now, his man smell and sounds having sent the shimmer of rose light into another world, her world of dream that he had somehow managed to share ever so briefly. Then she resented his presence in the woods, but the painting was lovely and when she looked from him back to the easel, he continued to speak with such kindness that finally she spoke too. She would never be able to remember a word that passed between them, only that some words did. And it wouldn't have mattered anyway if she could have recalled the innocence of their conversation, because the conversation between a woman a strange man is never innocent!

There had been a balmy humid warmth in the air when Stillbird awoke at dawn to see the painter, but as the sun reached higher in the sky it got dimmer and the air became cooler and soon a light snow began to fall, filling the air and sky with a thick, soft whiteness. Stillbird could glimpse the sun shining faintly and farther and farther off from her world, behind the slowly moving clouds of white. The snow outlined the black, bare branches that made graceful patterns against the sky and melted as it hit the silver creek that ran over and around varicolored rocks and tree roots. It was too beautiful to leave, and Stillbird spent the morning wandering in the first snow of the season, reluctant to go home.

Geese criss-crossed the sky, making the only sound in that muffled, foggy morning, and as she walked through a landscape that drifted in and out of the mist, Stillbird wondered again if the man she had seen was real or just a vision caught between sleep and awakening.

Only when she came within view of the house and the lean-to that served them as a barn did she know with certainty and a sickness of heart that the strange man was indeed real, for she saw him talking to Abel in front of the haystacks several hundred yards from the barn. Scanning the thick white sky, she found the pale circle of light that was the sun and realized she had been gone far too long, and that Abel would be worried about her and being worried, would be angry. She saw that Charlie was with him and expected the child's presence to calm him as she walked, not changing her pace, toward them. She thought she might pass them and stay on the road to the cabin, but Abel called to her, and when she got close enough to hear, she heard the strange man, the foolish man, address her and begin to talk about the morning. She said nothing and the man's words tapered off as he realized he was somewhere he didn't belong. He thanked Abel then, for directions perhaps? (Stillbird didn't know and couldn't ask) and begin to walk out of their lives as inconsequentially as he had wandered in.

No sooner had the painter headed off into the mountain than Abel began beating her. The man was still within her view but Stillbird was too proud to call out to him and knew instinctively that the stranger would be too afraid to interfere with a man who was beating his wife, maybe believing himself that she deserved it because of her conversation with him during the early morning mystery of the sunrise.

Stillbird endured Abel's beating in silence, feeling her soul join the geese that flew noisily overhead back and forth and back and forth, and she watched from a far distance as what started with a slap that knocked her down, ended with Abel kicking her prostrate body furiously. She curled up and tried to roll away from him on the wet rocky ground, but he followed her with his kicks and only quit when he heard Charlie crying. Then he yelled words of blame at her for what she had made him do in front of their son and carried the boy back to the house, running with him in his arms.

Stillbird lay beneath the sun, now high in the sky and burning through the morning fog and drying the earth and warming Stillbird, and she rested and waited for Abel to return and help her, but when no help came, she gathered her broken right arm in her left one, cradling it close to her broken ribs, drew her legs up under her, and stood slowly on those strong but shaky legs and walked slowly, deliberately, very carefully, every breath causing sharp pains in her side.

Abel watched her approach the house, and when she was close enough for him to see her holding her arm and the pallor of her face, he walked up the road to meet her and when he got close enough to see her grimace with pain and begin to swoon with it, he cried out and fell to his knees, holding her around her legs, which began to buckle. He stood and scooped her into his arms, crying as he carried her home. He told her how sorry he was and prayed to God to strike him dead if he ever did such a thing again, and Stillbird, hearing his words before she passed out with pain, realized it didn't matter if she believed him or not, because she had nowhere to go and a small child to care for.

Over time Stillbird learned to gauge the cycles of Abel's violence. As long as she herself was in pain, quiet and depressed, he treated her with a tender solicitousness, but when her own mood inexplicably elevated, his would plummet into morose anger that would eventually flare up in a sudden act of violence for any reason or no reason at all. Charlie would cry when it happened, sometimes bringing his father back to his senses, but then as he got more and more independent and himself endangered, Charlie would run away and avoid the anger that could as well be turned against him. He could see that his mother was helpless to stop it.

Spring, summer, fall, winter: each season bringing its own glorious beauty to the land, and Stillbird lost herself in their ebb and flow, walking night and day to find the earliest buds of color in the late March breezes that came warm from a far off sea, before winter's last brilliant blaze of ice and snow, and then finding the remnants of wet weather springs that dried up almost, but not quite, in the mid-summer, where she would steal a secret coolness from the entrance to vast caverns beneath their home, where puddled a few drops of sacred silver water. The autumn was her favorite time when she knew she could fly out of her body and drift back to ground with the leaves of unspeakable brightness; colors untethered to anything solid, like spirits gone wild with joy in the crisp air. This was the cause of the elation that surprised and angered Abel so often, so unfathomable, so resilient.

So the years passed and Abel was more often kind than cruel, but it was the cruelty that Stillbird got used to and the kindness that she feared. When he would leave for several days to trade in town and return with luxuriant satin and exquisite lace for Stillbird to make a dress that only he would see, she would begin to wait. Sometimes the blows would come even before the dress was finished, and she didn't mind if he tore her work to ribbons; just waiting for the storm to pass, her wounds to heal, a certainty of quiet now his fury was spent, and Stillbird weathered Abel through a dozen cycles of the seasons of the earth. At night when he lay on top of her, she dreamed she was buried and that wild things, flowers and lichens and mosses grew up through her and over her and protected her from any real violation. Abel's intensity never waned, but Charlie's childish affection wandered and he decided that his mother was plain crazy, talking only as she did to the deer and the birds in the woods. He was glad no one ever saw her; "the woman," as his father always called her, not knowing her real name (and Charlie not telling out of shame rather than a respect for the confidence his mother had long ago placed in him). "That crazy woman."

IV

That last day began warm and sunny, hot for one working hard in the sun. But toward afternoon, clouds drifted in and chilled the sun's warmth, and Stillbird came in early to build the fire in the hearth. She was nursing the coals and adding bits of bark and leaves, waiting for the blue flame, which always comforted her with its warmth and beauty, to flare, when a bobcat came close to the house and looked in at her. She stared back at the cat, afraid not of the cat, but of the omen that something terrible was about to happen. Then the cat was gone and Abel walked through the door telling her to wake up and that Charles was not home yet and he was worried. Charles had gone out that morning with a new horse and Abel was suspicious of the horse, probably because she loved it. It was a large rust-red mare with a spirit that the woman only vaguely remembered and recognized as her own.

Abel watched a while as Stillbird concentrated on the delicate work of encouraging the tiny flame and then he ordered her gruffly to go look for their son. So Stillbird quietly abandoned her task and her delight and went out to search for Charles in the woods. Shortly thereafter, Abel left to look as well, as he had intended to do. He had only ordered Stillbird out into the night because he was angry that she appeared to pay no attention to him, being busier with the fire than her husband. He walked out into the dusk, feeling anxious, feeling guilty and afraid God would punish him for something--he knew not what--through his beloved son.

As Stillbird walked through the woods, her eyes straining for signs of the kind of disturbance in the leaves or ground that a large horse would make, she saw the cat again, calmly feeding on the flesh of a fawn it had just killed. Stillbird smelled the blood even before she saw the cat, as it wafted intermittently through the chill air on faint waves of warmth from the earth. A hawk dipped and whirled overhead and disappeared with a cry into the clouds and circled back to hover over Stillbird as she made her slow and silent way through the woods. A crow and a magpie followed her as well just above the trees, flying in and out of the quickly descending mist. The sunset was a delicate tracery of gold outlining the thick, soft gray clouds that settled into the trees, an eerie close light reflected off damp leaves. Stillbird was reminded of a painting she could still see like yesterday, though she'd seen it last thirteen years ago. In the thick mountain mist, the dawn and the sunset appeared the same, exquisite and painful and always just out of reach of the earth-bound vision. There was glory behind the clouds and Stillbird yearned for it.

Stillbird took long, deep breaths of the cold air, but couldn't get the odor of fresh blood out of her nostrils, and she grew anxious and walked faster and faster until she was running and calling her son's name, but the only sound that came back to her in response was the call of the hawk, the scolding voice of the magpie and the unmistakable bark of geese she couldn't see. She stopped running and waited to let her ears adjust to the forest sounds, the creek and the movement of small animals. She walked toward the sound of the running water, and as she got closer, she distinguished her son's voice, crying and cursing, and then all of a sudden, as she scanned the trees, she saw his red shirt and came closer, but quietly, so he didn't hear or see her coming, and she watched him curse and beat the beautiful mare, angry because he had fallen and they were lost.

Stillbird, not wishing to frighten the horse more, was silent and sprang into the air and onto her son as he reached back with a willow switch in hand ready to strike. She held his arm firmly in her grasp, and he turned to look at her with tears like a child on his face. "Damn animal spooked and ran off with me." "The cat?" asked Stillbird…"I don't know. What difference? She needs to learn …" "She's was afraid of the mountain lion, she smelled the blood …" "She's an animal and she needs to learn and I'm going to teach her"…and Charles wrenched his arm free and began to beat the mare.

Stillbird jumped on him, silently still and held him to allow the mare to run, and then she pulled the switch from his hand when he turned to watch the horse run through the trees and beat him herself, shouting now, "See how that feels, see how that feels!" over and over until Abel came upon them and stopped her hand in mid-air and took the switch from her as she quieted down. There was silence then all around, for neither man had ever seen Stillbird raise her voice or exhibit rage. But then Abel, in his measured and cold way, told his wife that it was unseemly for a woman to beat her son who was a grown man, a man she should respect, and then he raised his arm with the switch, but stopped and handed the switch to his son, commanding the young man to beat the woman for her lack of respect. And Charles knew he couldn't do this to his mother, didn't want to do this to his mother, but Charles was afraid of his father and after the second command, he took the switch, and after the third command, given now with some heat, Charles struck her limply across her shoulders, his head down, his eyes and nose running, and she did not look at him either, but turned and walked away from the men, who turned and walked home.

The sun had set and they were lit now by the moon. Stillbird's heart beat with rage and a sense of freedom, for it was Charles who had kept her tied to Abel all those years, and now she would not stay to protect him. Abel's heart beat with righteousness and fear fighting inside of him, and Charles's heart nearly stopped with a loud, slow thud, as the world shrank small and dark around him, not even aware of when he walked inside the house and went to sleep, not sure where he woke the next day or what day it was. Charles was still in shock when his father told him at sunrise that he was going out to search for the woman. "The woman," he called her, had always called her. And Charles could only nod and curl up and go back to sleep, afraid to dream, afraid to wake...he slept for two full days, dreaming she was home again and the scene in the woods had not happened, but finally he had to wake up and work and eat and remember that it had happened. Charles didn't talk anymore, and Abel didn't expect him to; her son after all. Abel knew he'd done wrong, but couldn't say it and so he cursed the woman, but softly, under his breath, slower, until he was murmuring he knew not what, just murmuring to himself day in, day out, and day after day she didn't come back, and sometimes he went to search for her, and sometimes he simply prayed, and sometimes he murmured meaninglessly, forgetting where and who and when he was and forgetting the woman, until some animal reminded him of her, or the sunrise, or the sunset, or the autumn leaves as they turned. Sometimes he remembered Alwyn, and when he heard the geese overhead, he thought he was a child again back in Scotland. Without talking about it, his son began to take care of him, silently, sadly, finally a man.

Charles noticed when some things were taken from the cabin during the day while he and his father were out cutting wood, and he said nothing, hoping his father hadn't noticed. It happened from time to time, and once he was in the cabin and heard her and pretended to be sleeping, not wanting to know or to interfere.

Stillbird had walked back into the woods and found the bobcat, who had finished its meal, and followed it as it dragged the carcass to a cave from whence came a sweet water spring. It was necessary to crawl past the pool made by the spring to get into the large first room of the cave, and there the cat had dragged the bones of many animals, and Stillbird used these to make herself a fire and warm herself through the cold, early spring night. The cat brought more animals, leaving more meat on them, and Stillbird cooked the meat over the bones and ate, grateful for the gifts from the cat. She feared the cat might find and kill the rust-red mare, but the mare must have run very far away, for she never saw her again, and she knew that Charles hadn't found her either, and for that she was glad. She spied on her son and the man, Abel, and when they went into the forest to cut firewood, she crept back to the house and took some things she needed in the cave, some blankets and pots and bags of beans, a kerosene lamp and flints and some clothing. She wrapped it all in a blanket and put it on the sled made of the old sweat lodge poles, which she knew she would use for fuel the next winter. Not wishing to be seen during the day, she buried the sled with these things under piles of leaves that had accumulated over the years and marked the spot, so she could come back by night to retrieve them. In daylight it was necessary to move quickly and quietly and stay in the cave.

✢

One crisp autumn afternoon, Abel decided to go hunting, but he knew better than to suggest it to Charles, who had been treating him like a child now, ever since the woman had disappeared. It occurred to Abel that perhaps she had turned herself into an animal in the forest. The old Indian women were said to be able to do that, just like the witches in the stories from home. He'd even dreamed that he had wounded a doe and when he went to get her, she had already changed back into the woman, and he had carried her home and nursed her wound gently. It had hurt him to wake up that morning, because his dream had been so happy and peaceful at last. All his waking hours he felt an ache in his heart and his throat that made it hard to swallow food or talk without crying. No wonder his son treated him like a child. He simply did not understand love. He didn't know how to explain it.

So Abel left quietly with his bow and arrow and stalked her in the woods, and he found a doe and stood quietly, holding his breath, hoping she would not catch his scent. Slowly, slowly he raised his arm and took aim and let fly the arrow and hit her in the shoulder. The doe ran and he lost sight of her and had to stalk her again, sniffing the crisp air for the scent of blood, which he barely detected over the sweet wood smoke that wafted far into the forest from his home. Then he saw her standing quite still at the mouth of a cave, staring at a bobcat that had been attracted by the scent of her blood, and he watched as the cat killed the doe with his heart turned to stone, fearing that it was the woman the cat killed. He dreaded to see the cat mangle and devour the flesh of the magic animal, but he couldn't move and watched in wonder as the cat moved away without so much as touching her flesh. Abel began to move quietly and slowly toward the cave to examine the doe, but the cat came back and guarded her prey, and Abel understood he would be safe if he backed away, and he did and then ran home, his heart beating faster and faster, near to bursting. And then he was ashamed. He should have had faith, and the wood fairies would have protected him. The cat was a magic animal also, an evil witch, he was thinking in his child's mind, gone back now to that time he could never set right.

"Where have you been, father? I was so worried when I came down and you were gone. I've looked and called everywhere."

"I went hunting the woman, but I didn't save her. I was a coward and lost faith, and now she's dead and there is nothing I can do but bear my shame."

"Father, what are you talking about? What did you see and where did you go? How do you know that she is dead?"

"She turned herself into a doe, and I shot her with an arrow in the shoulder, just to wound her, not to kill her, and I would have brought her back home, but a mountain lion killed her, and I was afraid and ran home without her. She was at the entrance of a cave, and I am sure she has been living there, a woman by night and an animal by day. These Indians are magical like the fairies back home. Did I never tell you the stories?"

"Yes, father, you told me the stories, but we didn't believe those stories."

Then Charles noticed that his father looked beyond sad when he said he didn't believe in the stories, and he gently led his father to bed and promised to help him find the cave the next day. He sat by his father's bed and watched over him, until he was sure his father was asleep, and then he got up quietly to leave, but his father's voice called him back.

"Did I ever explain to you my love for your mother? Did I ever tell you how it was?"

"No, father, you never told me that." And Charles's heart sank, thinking what love had led to.

"It was like a story, too. A story I just remembered. I know I never told you this story, because I just remembered it now, but my mother told me this story a long time ago, before my brother was born. I'll tell you the story and you'll understand how I loved your mother.

"It was a story about a young Highland king who went to the forest to play games of strength with a fairy king and because he won, he got to take the fairy king's daughter as his wife, and then he won a horse that could fly, as you know those stories are full of horses that fly like the wind, faster even. But then he lost, and the fairy king made him promise to bring him something, a special sword, I think, and the flying horse helped him, because the horses in those stories could also talk, you know, and he took the sword to the king, but while he was gone on this adventure, a giant came and took his wife, whom he loved so much. Now that I think about it, that young king must have been like my brother, Jamie. You never knew Jamie of course. He died the night you were conceived. That shocks you doesn't it? Did you know that your mother was married first to my brother? Well, I guess I am like the giant in the story.

The poor giant that no one knew anything about. In the story, they kill the giant and everyone is glad about it. But the giant had a soul. He kept it hidden in a special place, and that was the second part of the story. How they killed the giant by finding his soul."

Abel fell silent then, almost asleep with weariness, and Charles went closer to him and put his hand on his father's forehead and told him to sleep now and they would talk about the story tomorrow. But his father said no, he would finish the story now, just let him doze a moment, so Charles waited, and his father closed his eyes and rested, but spoke slowly and finished the story about the giant's soul.

"The young king was able to find his bride where the giant had hidden her in a large cave, because his horse helped him, a fairy horse, you know, and when he got there, the giant was gone and the other horses there hid him beneath their legs. Oh, then there was more that I won't tell you, how the giant would come home each night exhausted and feed the horses who would bite and kick at him, and how he would tell his woman that had he but had his soul in his body, they would have killed him. Each night he would tell her that, and she would ask him where his soul was, and he would tell her something different, but finally he told her the truth about where his soul was hidden. I remember this, because when I was little I thought it was so funny. I didn't really understand the story then, you see. The poor giant's soul was hidden in an egg inside a duck, which was in the belly of a sheep, and the sheep was buried beneath a rock in the cave. We laughed, my mother and I, when she told this part. And she told it well, long and making quite a play of it. So when the giant was gone, the young king and his beautiful fairy wife dug up the sheep, which ran from them, but the king called a dog, who caught the sheep, and they cut it open and found the duck, who flew away, but the king called a hawk, who caught the duck, and they cut it open and found the egg, which rolled into the river, but the king called an otter, who brought them the egg, and the fairy wife broke the egg, and that broke the soul of the giant, who died somewhere out there; somewhere, no one knew where or cared. He never came back and the young king and his wife were glad. So, you see, my love was like the giant's soul, hidden, so well hidden, but now it's been broken, and I am dying. You can see that can't you?"

"We'll find her father, I'll help you. We'll make amends, I promise."

But Abel didn't hear his son's promise, because he was already sleeping the deep, sound sleep of total exhaustion.

✢

During the first few days in the cave, Stillbird noticed that birds came and roosted in trees nearby: an owl at night to warn her when death would come to visit her and various crows who took turns guarding her by day, to warn her, when she ventured out of the cave, of the men who might pass by and find her. When she heard their warning cries, she hurried to hide herself down among rock outcroppings or behind the upended root systems of fallen trees, overgrown with mosses, clutching rocks in twisted, grasping root fingers and protecting Stillbird, now a child of the earth as completely as her mother ever dreamed. As Stillbird grew bolder and wandered farther from her cave by day and night, the crows followed, watching over her as they did their own young. Once, in mid-summer, when she fell asleep in the warm afternoon sun in a field of tall grass, and Charles wandered very near to her, the crows all flocked to her and landed on her body, dozens of them, to hide her sleeping form from the man, and he went his way, not understanding the birds, not even listening to them. Abel might have guessed what they were about, but Abel still sat in the rocker back at the cabin, barely eating, preparing for death, recalling each day of his life, slowly and carefully.

✣

His father tricked him. Jamie was in the cupboard, and Alwyn lay crying, curled up in a protective ball, keeping even her tears secret, and Abel had run and hidden inside the hollow of an ancient, nearly dead oak tree not far from the house. He could hear his father crying, "Don't leave me alone!" And there was such pain in his father's cry that he, Abel, had been moved to immeasurable sadness and left his hiding place to go comfort his father, who was sorry for beating his mother. He came up behind him and hugged him around his knees and his father was surprised and stank from whiskey, and crying still and for a while he spoke tearfully to Abel, sorry for himself and wanting Abel to understand his loneliness, but then he remembered that Abel had run from him and hidden himself and left him alone, and he got angry again and beat Abel too, leaving bruises all over his arms and legs, and later when Abel would look at the bruises, he couldn't understand how his father could be so sad and so angry at the same time. His father had finally left, and Abel had curled up next to Alwyn and touched her, and they cried together and held each other. Even as he hated to remember the fear and confusion about his father, Abel cherished the memory of his mother holding him and the two of them sobbing together, more together than they would ever be in simple conversation. When Abel remembered this, he sobbed again and held himself as he rocked back and forth, unaware of Charles watching him. Charles could do nothing but watch his father's grief.

The crows surrounded the house each afternoon in summer, eating the elderberries that grew like weeds up against the windows even against the loft. Noiselessly they ate and watched and listened and heard nothing but the steady rocking and occasional sobs, the only thing left of Abel's voice. Charles walked all over their land and beyond into the woods, and the crows would take flight, leaving the elderberry bushes one by one to follow high overhead, watching the farm, the village, all the people all at once, as they moved around each other in a mystical dance, the steps dictated by a twisted instinct, and only the crows could see the patterns they made.

As the summer drew near its end, Stillbird gathered wild berries and apples and other fruits that grew here and there as well as the wild onions and watercress and mint that had grown in abundance since spring. In the last beautiful days of autumn, she found a doe killed, but otherwise untouched, outside the entrance to the cave, and she labored all day to skin the animal and slice off the meat in thin strips that she hung to dry in the cave over a smokey fire. And she stored up the sunlight in her body, up and out before dawn to watch the mountains emerge from the mists, with an excitement that felt like youth, and lingered outside long after dusk, rejoicing in the crisp clearness of the evening air, the sharpness of the moonlit trees that reached graceful beyond their few remaining leaves, cutting the infinite sky into myriad shapes that fascinated her eye. Stillbird reached out her own arms in a quiet dance that imitated the trees, and the wind and the years fell away from her, memories of years and years with Abel and Charles forgotten, meaningless now. Her spirit was free and memory didn't matter. Once clenched around her child, her arms now opened by themselves and felt like powerful wings as she moved them around and around and let her body follow. Then she would collapse into piles of leaves and smell the air, fighting sleep, not wanting to miss the beauty of the night.

After Abel told Charles the story of the giant's hidden soul, he struggled to remember everything, every day of his life, for there were more memories than he had thought about throughout the summer and fall and he knew he would die soon and he wanted to say good-bye to his life and all of his memories, the bad as well as the good, for they were all he had of love and companionship; just those memories of his mother and father and his brother, Jamie and a few others who came and went briefly in the story of his life. To Charles, he must have appeared in a silent shock, an open-eyed sleep, but he was working hard not to forget a single day, a single word. He knew by now that he could die any time, but he wanted to get ready and do it right, not like Jamie or his mother--rushed out of life so suddenly and without warning. And he wanted to apologize to God for the mistakes he had made, and he expected God to convey his apologies to the woman. He saw her often living in a cave, and he was certain she lived in the cave where the cat had killed the doe, but he knew he couldn't go there, and now he didn't even want to try. He just wanted to think it all out and die. Once he tried to tell Charles and talk to Charles, but whenever he spoke of death, his son bid him sleep and rest and promised to do things--find the woman, make amends--and Abel realized that Charles didn't understand that that was what he was doing and that it was nearly over. He felt sorry for Charles, but had nothing to give Charles that Charles could understand, and it was too late now. Charles still didn't believe in the stories, and Abel realized that the young don't really believe in death either, and only when a man believes in death, can he then believe in the stories. And then all reality changes. Anger had been Abel's reality and now he had none left. He was not even angry that for all the times he had remembered Alwyn, she never came to him in dreams to tell him what death was like. He would know soon enough. And he knew he would not visit Charles either to tell his son about death. He paid no more attention to Charles, and even left the cabin with renewed energy to wander in the woods just to get away from his son's voice, because it was the voice of the living, and Abel was yearning for the magic voices of the stories, the fairies and the magical animals and Stillbird, if he could find her. He would not look but thought she would come to him if he became a part of the stories. Abel prayed that there was no soul to live on after the death of the body and yearn eternally, for then he knew he would yearn always after Stillbird, and wanted to believe that they two could rest somehow together, without desire or rejection, without anger or even love, just the comfort of a shared sleep. So Abel prepared by thinking of each thing he had to think of, just once so he could throw it away and empty his mind, his soul, and rest.

That winter was mild but late, even after the buds had grown bright and ebullient upon the trees, there was one last long snowstorm. The world was buried so deep within the snow that it seemed a peaceful, silent blank, and Abel's mind as well went blank until the snow thawed and the streams overflowed their banks, flooding the fields and the roads, coming up so close to the cabin that Abel thought he looked out upon a lake. He remembered then following his mother to a lake where he had watched the geese and watched while she walked right into the middle of it, and with a dance-like movement, twirled down into the water and lay there. It was early spring then, too, and still quite cold. She would not drown, but surely she would freeze.

V

It was a silent scene that played itself out in Abel's mind, he could feel the cold, feel the peacefulness, feel in fact the calm lethargy that overtook his mother as she lay in the lake. He had to struggle to remember his own feelings then, and what he had done, and what he had said, and then her words to him. He had to rouse himself to feel the life in his limbs to remember how he had run down to the lake and into the water to his mother, and he had tried to lift her out of the water, and she had refused at first to let him lift her out of the freezing water and told him slowly, sluggishly, almost asleep, that she had had enough of life. "But what about me and Jamie?" he had asked her desperately. And she had said then, even as she moved to rise out of the water, "Oh you are old enough to take care of yourself…" and by then she was standing…"but you are right about Jamie…he is too young and it would be too hard for you to care for him alone." And she allowed Abel to help her as she stumbled a little getting up out of the water and began walking back, shivering now, she was back among the living. They shivered and huddled together and once home, he wrapped her in a blanket and built a fire and it was just the two of them while Jamie slept. The man had long since gone and was not coming back. That they knew.

And then it was over, the long, sad litany of days. Abel went out, paying no attention to the cold water he tramped through, his body no longer mattered. He just walked and walked following the creek bed as best he could in the flooded landscape.

✣

With her needs for warmth and food being, almost miraculously, met all through the winter, Stillbird had given herself over to the long hibernation of animals, sleeping through entire days when it was cold or wet outside, and only leaving the cave on the warmest days to trek through the woods, confident now that the crows would screech a warning to her should any human being approach. She even hiked back to the cabin for supplies on a couple of occasions and often walked to the rock and the oak tree where Jamie was buried. She barely remembered him now. Only the birds flying high overhead could see how closely Stillbird and Abel and Charles circled each other, never seeing each other, although Stillbird sometimes caught the odor of the men on the wind when they passed nearby to hunt or cut wood. He monthlies had dried up completely and with that change, her sense of smell became as keen as a dog's.

In early March, Stillbird could smell the change of the season, a soft humidity in the air, that balmy scent and feel that precedes the last winter storms. The buds that she had to get right up close to to see in January and February were now fat and colorful, pink and pale green and yellow, creating a cloud of lace around the graceful limbs of trees and the tangle of low-growing bushes that grew up in the patches of light, where the taller trees had been cut for firewood and timber to build cabins. The branches seemed to dance to a tune Stillbird heard faintly at the very edge of her consciousness, and she was sure they moved around on the hills at dusk, coming closer to surround her and protect her. Everywhere she walked, she felt nurtured by the hills and the trees, as she did by the cave itself and the creek that flowed into the forest from the mouth of the cave. Living at the source of all the water in the region, Stillbird often dreamed of floating down the creek, letting it carry her through the forest, the hills, past cabins and farmsteads and fields of grass where cattle grazed, and gardens, all kinds of gardens.

Each year of her life with Abel and Charles, she had grown a different garden, placing the vegetables in different spots mixed with flowers, sometimes in rows, sometimes in circles, sometimes in patches. She remembered, as if she watched someone else, a child perhaps, running up to the loft to look out a small window Abel had cut under the eaves, at the design of her garden.

She had stopped her nightly walks after the incident with the painter, but she soon became as immersed in her garden, making a kind of painting of it the way she arranged the tomatoes, the marigolds, the yellow squash in with the pale or darker shades of green of lettuce and peas and potatoes.

One spring she would ring the garden with the tall corn, another she would plant it in a cross through the middle. She had been lucky in the site of the garden, with its endlessly sweet soil, the most hours of sunlight and a strong year-round spring just up the hill, so it was easy to irrigate when the summer rains didn't come on time. So Stillbird dreamed also of gardens. In March she would be planting onions and kale, peas and lettuce, and they would be eating fresh greens even before she put in the tomato plants, nurtured along in a window in the sun, before being arranged in their part of her overall design, usually next to or alternating with marigolds, which she planted to keep certain bugs away, and because she loved the smell of them. Even the tiniest little growth of marigold left a strong, good smell on her hands. Later she would harvest them when she harvested the vegetables and use them to make a dye for yarn she spun from wool that Peter sometimes brought for her; a gift from his mother, who sent messages, but never visited in person. Stillbird tried to remember if she had ever seen the woman. It amazed her to realize some nights when she woke from hours of sleep that there were events in her life that she had forgotten almost completely, and then couldn't decide if she remembered or imagined them. Had there ever been a painter emerging from a morning mist in an early spring snowstorm? What had happened then? Had they talked? About what? What had he looked like? She vaguely remembered Abel in this scene, but shadowy, as if he kept his face averted from her. In fact, she couldn't remember Abel's face clearly at all, and she was relieved, because she didn't want his face haunting her dreams.

Often Stillbird dreamed she was in the bottom of a boat, a strange dream for her, because she couldn't remember ever being in a boat, or near a body of water large enough to float one, but she dreamed this many times, more than she could count during the winter and early spring. It was dark, for the boat was covered, and she lay in the very bottom where it curved down toward the center, and it rocked her peacefully back and forth from side to side and she would sleep and then she would smell the water that leaked into the boat and she would be afraid, but then not afraid, as the water rose to her feet and the side that she lay on, and it was warm and soon she would be covered in a blanket of warm water, rocking and sleeping. Then she would wake and smell the spring that rose from deep in the earth and flowed out from the cave entrance into the hills and the forest, and just by the cave opening, she could smell an abundance of watercress and moss and mint. She ate the watercress and the mint, but the earth itself, laced with the roots of these plants, smelled so good she wanted to eat the very mud, and sometimes she would taste it and swallow just a little, making her feel warm and satisfied even when other foods were scarce. Stillbird then remembered eating earth when she was a child and her mother had scolded her, but her grandmother--she was sure it was her grandmother--had laughed and told her that a little dirt never hurt any baby. But the woman had died before Stillbird had learned to talk, even to say the word grandmother. Stillbird remembered her grandmother for the first time when she ate the mud from the cave spring. And then, as the taste of the earth disappeared, so did the memory. She went back to sleep, awoke in the dark and saw the moon shining into her hiding place and slept again until the sun was high and hot in the sky.

Some nights Stillbird awoke to see an animal outlined against the moonlight--a bear, or a deer, or the cat. Somehow she knew it was the same cat she saw from time to time.

One day it was hot enough to bathe in the creek, the next, a soft, light snow began to fall. Stillbird hiked back to her cave, still smelling of the flowers she had caressed, snowflakes sparkling in her hair, and there she wrapped herself in a blanket and sat in the entrance watching the earth pale and glisten. The beauty of it took her breath away, and she didn't notice the cold. The sun didn't set in a brilliant display of color, but simply disappeared into the afternoon whiteness, and the sky darkened gradually into oblivion. Stillbird felt her way to her bed by the hearth, where the fire smoldered, always waiting to be blown into flame, and fed with new wood, new bones. This time Stillbird was followed by the cat, who no longer frightened her. "Grandmother," she whispered, and the cat followed quietly to lay down beside her and keep her warm through the last spring storm.

The cat dreamed of running over endlessly flat plains of billowing golden grasses, into a golden horizon, after a large and thunderous herd that she couldn't see but could smell getting closer and closer. Stillbird dreamed that she was borne along as fast as wind, on the back of the cat, through that same land, and then the cat turned into the rust-red mare and they leaped over a wide, flat river, and then she became the cat, prowling the forest, sniffing out the mare, stalking the mare, and then it was a woman she found, bloody and dead in the cave, and Stillbird realized, still dreaming, that she was all of them. Still dreaming, Stillbird felt herself become the crow and flew higher and higher and watched herself and the mare and the cat, and she felt only movement, thought only movement, as she danced in the air, twirling, twirling, borne in dizzying circles on currents of air, currents of river water. She never stopped dreaming.

✤

For three days and three nights the soft, light snow fell quietly and steadfastly, burying the earth, the cabin, the river and rocks. Abel never stopped rocking, soothed by the movement as his memories slowed and stopped. Charles went out walking in the fairy-tale whiteness, rainbows glittering off every tree, and he took his bow and arrows, not wishing to disturb the silence of that lovely white world, and he shot a deer and followed the path of red blood on the white snow, until he found the animal still running, but slower, and he shot a second time and brought her down. He hoisted the doe over his shoulders and stumbled back to the cabin with the food, but his father would not eat, and Charles cut and cooked the meat with a heavy heart and a slow hand. He tried to interest Abel in telling him more stories from Scotland, but Abel was done now with the stories, all of them, so Charles instead told Abel stories, reminding him of the old country and old people and searching his own memory for what his father had told him over the years. He tried to think of funny ones, but when he tried to laugh all alone, he found himself crying.

"Remember, father, you told me that the ocean voyage from Scotland to New York took forty days and forty nights, and you felt like you were on Noah's ark. But all the animals that had been brought on two by two were slaughtered four by four to feed the crew and the passengers. Sick of the stringy goat meat, you were, after forty days of it, you told me. Do you remember that?"

But Abel sat still and quiet, as if the soft falling snow had buried his heart and his mind as it had buried the cabin. It was dark in the cabin with the windows all covered with snow and frost, even when the sun shone brightly outside, and Charles felt as if he lived inside a cave and walked out often into the bright day to remind himself he still lived at all.

And then it stopped snowing and the sun worked on the mounds of snow that covered the world, melting it into lakes and puddles and streams. Where the earth was porous, the melted snow seeped down into it, and where it was bedrock, the melted snow washed down the rock into gullies and sinkholes, and the spring waters, hidden deep within the earth, rose up to meet the snow waters, and the little cabin seemed like a small ark to Charles, where he felt safe, but he was afraid for his mother, who had disappeared into the world of magic animals and forest and unpredictable waters that sank into the earth and rose again as floods upon its surface. Charles was afraid to go looking for her, but Abel, silently without a word of his intent, went out into the flood, steadily, thoughtlessly, plodding along the side of what had been the creek, finding his way by instinct and habit as surefooted as if in a trance, and indeed Charles thought he might be entranced. Charles tried to follow his father to protect him, but soon realized he couldn't and his father didn't need him.

The water came in so suddenly with a rush, through the large front entrance of the cave, and Stillbird could not seek to escape in the face of its strength. She crept and climbed to another opening, knowing it would be a tight fit that would let her out in a large sinkhole in the woods. Once, while exploring, she had gotten into the cave that way, but had barely gotten out again because her body didn't bend to conform to the innards of the cave at that end. She'd known terror that time. But the water caught up with her and washed her toward the tight sinkhole exit. She could see the rock formations of the cave spin by her by the light from the hole and she panicked as she was pushed closer to its harsh edges, fearing to be crushed. But the water washed her out of the cave, as her body and limbs were bent around outcroppings of rock and slid along the mud out into the deep and wide impression on the outside. She had forced herself to be calm and let her body and limbs float in the rush of water, but the water had filled her up inside and the pressure from within and without was painful, unbearable, worse than giving birth, and it occurred to her that perhaps this was what birth was like, and she realized that the earth that had nurtured her in the dark womb of the cave was now giving her up to another life.

Stillbird exploded with pain and broke free and pushed her spirit bodyless and swam and flew into the trees, the clouds, hiding among them and looking down at the woman's body that roiled around in the flooded sinkhole before being pushed again over rocks and tree roots and an old creek bed that was usually dried up, but now overflowed its banks and spilled over the deer paths and cowpaths that flanked it.

Downstream the body tumbled, into the woods and toward Abel's homestead.

Stillbird slept the sleep of the newborn and woke again, startled by the cries of a woman in pain. But she was in a house now and as Stillbird looked closer, she saw this was not the woman she had been, but a stranger, a woman not her, but like her, who was struggling to give birth to a large boy child, who seemed to be dying in the process. There were people around her talking to her, trying to help her, but they didn't see Stillbird, who drifted close to the woman's ear and whispered, then, realizing only the woman could hear, shouted words of instruction and encouragement. Stillbird breathed in and out with the woman as she guided her, now breathe, now push…and the woman rallied and fought hard and pushed her baby out, and then, when the baby boy was washed and laid upon her breast to nurse, she looked around for the voice, moving only her eyes. She saw her husband and his relief and her sister and her relief, but she didn't see the other, and she thought she must be gone, but then she heard the voice, and the voice said, "It's all over now and you are fine. You can rest now." "Forever?" asked the mother, no longer young, no longer strong, no longer brave. "Forever," said the voice, and the woman followed that sweet voice to a rest she knew she'd earned, breathing in and letting it out slow and peaceful one last time as her baby nursed at her breast.

When John Banks felt his mother's milk stop coming, he began to howl, and his father and aunt came running to see what had happened and found Amelie Banks dead at last, and they lifted the baby from her breast, mixing their cries with his and with the soothing sounds people make to try to stop the cries of infants. They named the baby John and said he was a miracle baby, born at the very edge of death.

✢

When Abel found his wife's body, her lungs swam in river water and mud and her arms and legs were scraped and broken and bloated with water, wrapped around the roots of a tree that had been brought down by the rushing river. Nonetheless, he longed to keep her with him and he chipped away at the ice that had formed around her body with his own bare hands. Gently he pulled her fingers and hair from the ice and lifted her body from the creek. He carried her back to the cabin and sat her body in the rocker and tried to dress her in the cream-colored satin and lace he had bought a year before in anticipation of her return. Charles came home and found his father in this hopeless endeavor and talked gently to his father, but when his father didn't appear to hear him, Charles shouted at the man, who still didn't hear him, but kept on working with the body and the satin and the lace, and finally Charles slapped his father, but Abel barely noticed even that and only cried softly, while Charles told him they must bury her. In the end, Abel couldn't help and Charles buried her alone, leaving a wooden cross to mark the spot until he could get a stone. The next day he dragged his father into town to help him choose and load a stone onto their wagon for the grave, and the two men, one working as mechanically as a machine, set the stone at her grave just as the sun set, a rare and bright magenta, and Abel remarked it was a passionate color in the sky that evening and asked his son for his mother's name, for she had never told him her Indian name, and she had never allowed him to call her Rosie.

Now it was Charles who couldn't speak and his father would die never knowing the name of the woman he had loved. They walked back to the house, but Abel would not go in. He said goodnight to his son, and those were his last words to anyone. Then he found the ancient oak tree that leaned perpetually into the large boulder, caught between life and death, and he wedged himself into the spot where he had first awaited Rosie 18 years ago and in his mind he counted each fall, each winter, each spring and each summer of her life as he remembered it, feeling her pain now on top of his own. He fell asleep and awoke only when Charles came looking for him and found him huddled against the rock like a runaway child and lifted him out and helped him stumble back to the house. There, Abel rocked back and forth in the chair that was her chair, knowing it was over, that he had counted each day, his days and hers too, and he ate nothing, drank nothing, just counting them, those days they had shared until he died, just before Charles was about to tell about the snake on the porch on a long ago summer evening. This was his penance, his amends to her, and he felt forgiven.

It was an aging Peter who helped Charles load a second grave stone in his wagon and center it at the head of the grave dug next to Stillbird's. After carving Abel's name, birthdate and date of death, Charles carved a small bird into his mother's blank stone, just the tiny bird, no words or dates, and then he enfolded his hard-muscled body around the hard granite, nearly blank but for the small, secret figure, and he cried and cried, gripping the stone tightly, the way an infant clings to its mother's body in a world too large and new.

Charles was 17, the same age his uncle Jamie had been when he had lost his mother, and had to leave Scotland to come to a new land. Abel and Jamie had traveled from New York to Virginia their first year in the new land, and thence to the southwest mountains of West Virginia. Abel had told Charles about those days when Charles was just old enough to begin exploring their own farmstead, and often thereafter, he would ask his father to tell him again and tell him more, so he had a mental map of places he longed to see and how to get there. He might even go to Scotland. He decided he'd get a job on a ship and wander until he felt at home. But at the same time he knew he'd miss this home, and the day after he buried his father, he was up at dawn to watch the mist lift from the hills, and he memorized every mood of the landscape from dawn until darkest night and walked every mile of the county, slowly and carefully storing up memories for the next phase of his life as he imagined it would be, lonely and dangerous and, of course, mysterious, like the fairy tales his father had told him, almost right up to the end.

Charles had no trouble finding a couple to purchase his land and the cabin. What he needed was cash and a horse to carry him far away. He had meant to bury the satins and laces that his father had bought for his mother, but had forgotten because of grief and the need to worry about his father, so he was embarrassed when the wife found those fine fabrics and the pieces of torn dresses and looked at him with curiosity. Blushing with shame he took the pile out of her arms and disappeared into the woods and laid the laces and satins one by one on top of her grave, and then he lay down to sleep a while in the late afternoon sun and awakened with the evening chill, and a light rain fell upon him. He left the graves then and went directly to his horse. The cash was in his jacket, and he rode down the mountains toward Roanoke, while the woman watched from the porch, curious still.

Part II

John Banks

VI

He was an odd figure, dressed in a preacher's collar, but with knee-high boots made of suede like Indians wore and a wide brimmed hat that looked like he'd gotten it from a theater's costume room. He wore a pendant with a cross and a circle hanging from it and carried a briefcase with frayed corners that showed glimpses of what was inside; mostly magazines and newspapers, tabloids with colorful sensational headlines. He had an interesting face that would have been handsome, but for the costume that pegged him immediately as insane.

He preached on street corners in the late afternoon as workers came out of office buildings headed for trolleys and buses. He knew if he preached near the stops that folks would have to listen while they waited for the next bus or streetcar, they couldn't avoid him by walking away. He carried a shallow plate in his briefcase that he'd pass around and accept donations with a preacher's dignity, saying quietly, "for the shelter," as if he were raising money for a shelter for the homeless. In fact he was raising money for his own night's lodging, usually in a shelter of some kind, and a little extra for some wine to warm his bones. On those occasions he collected more than he needed for the night's drink and lodging, he'd give it away to the men he found there, drunk as he would be by then; drink helping them all to find hope and piety. He could afford to be generous, knowing that what he didn't give away could be easily stolen from him.

Once, he'd gotten the idea of saving his cash for a bus ticket to Florida, being too old and sick now to tolerate the cold winds and snow of Charleston, West Virginia, but the first night he fell asleep with cash on him, he awoke to find it gone--and to think he'd denied himself his usual bottle of wine before bed in the interest of getting to Florida that much sooner. So he learned yet another lesson just when he thought he couldn't learn anymore, not from God or life.

Some on the street called him John the Baptist, because of a story he told of the second coming, saving a young girl that was pregnant with the son of God, a miracle, he said, and cried and cried, while those who had stayed in the alleys, bars and shelter to listen laughed and called him crazy. "Oh yes, that's what they all said, said I was crazy, said the child was the child of the devil, abandoned me and said I was crazy." And he'd just cry himself to asleep those nights. The first time he got drunk and told his story, he was new on the streets of downtown Charleston and was run off by the men who had taken over the alleys and doorways after dark. But he stuck and soon he was an old-timer and tolerated, even respected for his consistency. He had other stories too, got lost often in the landscape of too many memories and too many places, towns and hollers throughout the state and the ocean, too, for John had traveled in his day as far as the ocean to the east and the gulf coast to the southwest. He'd done his share of wandering in the world, and in his mind, too.

Now was wartime and all the news was about Pearl Harbor, a place John, or JB, as his nickname had been shortened to, had never heard of. And the streets were full of men in uniform, which reminded him of his younger days, and sometimes he thought he was a young man again, and when the soldiers talked about going to France, he remembered that other war, not that long ago. Not enough years have gone by, thought JB, for there to be another war. It must be the first one, and he must be re-living those days because he was dying, and sure indeed, John Banks was dying, day by day, night by night, bottle by bottle and pain by pain as he thought about the days gone by. "I think," he told a young soldier, "I think we are born and we start in to dying right then and there, right from the first day of our lives, we are dying, day by day." The soldier didn't listen to that; it wasn't what he wanted to hear. "Pray for me old man," he asked and gave JB a handful of greenbacks. JB gave them back, or tried to.

"Too much money," he said. "I'm just trying to help you old man," said the soldier. "Oh, but you'll learn young man, when you try to help people, you just end up hurting them more. Understand?"

"No. I don't understand that. What's the matter with you? You act like a preacher out here. I've heard you, calling the people to Christ. Don't you believe in helping people? I'm going off to war to help my country, don't you believe in that?"

"Don't know about war, son. Don't know what to tell you about war. I guess you got to go. They put you in jail anyway if you don't. But if you'll go inside this here bar where it's warm and buy me a drink, I'll tell you about a lesson I learned about helping people."

"Why do you need to get warm? It isn't cold now. What's the matter with you?"

"Son, I get so cold in the winter, I never do warm up. Even the littlest breeze reminds my bones of the chill buried deep inside them. I got to bake my bones in Florida some day to really get warm. I bin to the ocean up in Virginia and I bin to Florida--both sides of it, the ocean and the gulf--and all around the gulf coast from Florida to Texas, and if you weren't going off to war, I'd tell you all about it, maybe let you buy me a bus ticket and we could ride and talk and have a few beers, us two, but you are going, maybe even tonight, I don't know, you haven't told me, but if you got a minute or two, I can tell you about this one thing, this lesson I learned about helping folks."

The soldier, no more than 18 or 19 years old, looked at his watch and said he had a couple of hours actually and might as well get him a bite if they had some soup, or maybe the turkey special, as he looked up and read the card in the window, and the two men went inside in the dark, narrow bar with a few booths, and they took a booth so the kid could eat his turkey special and JB told him about one of the lessons he'd learned.

"A Negro family moved into our county when I was about twelve years old. I'd never seen Negroes before but from a distance, not to know them, you know what I mean? Anyway, my daddy, he told me to stay away from them, but when I asked why, he couldn't give me a good answer, and I was at that age I wanted reasons for everything, like there could be reasons for everything. Something else I learned was there are not reasons for most human behavior. Well, anyway, I got to be friendly with the boy in the family that was about my age, and I think my daddy knew but didn't pay attention, he just waiting, you know, for something to happen so he could say, 'I told you so,' something like that.

"That first harvest for them, things didn't go well. Seems some animals got into their crops and ate up most of what they'd planted for cash, and they was looking at a harsh winter with no money, and I wanted to help them some way. Only way I could think of to help the family was to give them some of our food that my aunt had canned. She had hundreds of canned vegetables and meats in the root cellar, and I didn't think she'd miss it if we were careful to take some cans from the back rows, some from here, some from there, not leave any big holes, you understand. That boy, I'll never forget his name, Ruben was his name, and Ruben, he didn't want to do this, but I could see his brothers and sisters and Ruben himself were hungry most of the time, all skinny and looking hungry, so I kept at him. 'She'll never miss it,' I told him.

"Old Andrew, who helped Daddy on the farm, saw us stealing the food one night, and I prayed he wouldn't say nothing. I knew Andrew had a soft spot for me because he'd been in love with my ma, so the rumor went. He probably wouldn't have said nothing, but my auntie did miss those cans. I think she musta counted them every day, like a miser with his money. And she raised such a fuss that my daddy had to do something to keep her quiet. I didn't know what to do, because if I confessed, they'd want the cans back and they'd wonder why I'd be stealing from my own house, you know, so I kept quiet and hoped Andrew wouldn't talk, but he did. Told me later he had to, or they'd have thought it was him. What Andrew said wasn't the whole truth, though. He said he saw the nigger boy stealing the food and he didn't mention me at all. So my daddy went and got that boy and brought him back to our farm, did it while the parents were out cutting and gathering wood for the winter. He said to me, 'See what you done? Playing with a nigger, and now he knows where everything is that has value and he can steal whatever he wants. But I'm going to teach him a lesson so he won't never come back here again.' Well, here is where the hard lesson comes in. You see, I was afeared of my daddy, but I knew I had to do the right thing in the eyes of the Lord, so I up and confessed that it was my idea and that Ruben would never have done it, but for me telling him over and over, and I was thinking as I said it that I would bear my punishment like a man, not utter a sound. But my daddy only said that I didn't know what I was talking about and me already twelve and begun to preaching Sundays, and I argued with him. But he told Andrew to take me outa there and Andrew grabbed me and hauled me away, kicking and screaming like a baby. I thought Andrew had lied to protect me and I resented him for that because I didn't need his protection. But it wasn't me he was protecting. He was protecting the way things were, protecting my daddy from getting even angrier than he was because he knew my daddy needed to believe that we were better than the Negroes, and that his son was better than the Negro boy. I was trying to explain things to Andrew whilst he was dragging me away, and he wasn't listening, because he knew it didn't matter anyway, and I kept thinking if I screamed it louder he'd hear the truth, but he shushed me and then he said the thing that made me forgive him and forgive God and keep on preaching a while even after that first hard lesson. He said, 'As long as you keep on screaming, your daddy will keep on whipping the poor nigger boy and he ain't screaming at all.' And he turned me around to see, and I shut my mouth then, and my daddy did stop whipping him, but it was too late. Ruben dropped to the ground like a rag doll with all its stuffing taken out, and my daddy just up and left him there. Andrew let go of me and went to wash and bandage that boy's cuts and my daddy didn't go near them, and Andrew, not knowing what else to do for him, gave the boy a drink of whiskey to dull the pain and get him on his feet and out of the way. That's what happened, and I realized that it was me my daddy was teaching the lesson to. So you see, sometimes you want to help folks and just end up hurting them instead, and that is the way of it. I learned then all we can do is beg the Lord to have mercy on us and don't even try to understand, because this world don't make no sense to just a man."

The soldier had finished eating and looked at his watch, thinking that the old man was done, but JB shook his head as if it were heavy with wisdom and asked for another beer and a shot of scotch, if he didn't mind and went right on talking.

"I wasn't done learning, though, cause then I commenced to begging for a miracle instead of just mercy. I still wanted too much. It was my birthright, so to speak. You see, my poor ma should've died with me still in her belly, but she hung on just long enough to give birth to me, and my auntie and my daddy called me a miraculous child, and I just figured I was entitled to another miracle, just one, something that I could do myself. I always heard voices, and I was sure one of them must have been God speaking to me, and that was why I started in to preaching when I was just a child, maybe eleven, almost twelve, just before the Negro family moved into the county. I never practiced what I would say, but just let the voice of God guide me, and sure enough, something always came up and people would get all excited, more excited listening to me than the older preachers who came through the county, and next thing you knew, I was traveling myself, all over the state and then all over the south. I didn't worry about how I would live because I had faith that God would provide, and he always did. The people would fight among themselves over who would have me to dinner and give me a bed to sleep in, and they gave me money when they had next to nothing themselves, and some tried to give me the food from their gardens they'd put up, and I had a hard time refusing, but I hated to take those canned goods, remembering what happened to Ruben, so I would take them and then give them away the next place I stopped. I had a wagon and a good horse and that's how I traveled, and many's the night I slept in the wagon by some river and I loved that, I loved the outdoors and sleeping outdoors when it was a clear night, and I could just open my eyes and see the stars filling up the sky. I loved that more than anything else about my life, and it was a prayer that I didn't have to speak, a silent, unspoken, almost unthought prayer just looking at those stars, the work of the Lord and loving it.

"It was when I was sleeping in my wagon by a river that the miracle happened, and even though it all went bad after a time, it was a glorious few months for me back then. It was 1928 in the springtime. I remember, because I had just been home to celebrate my 28th birthday with my old auntie and my daddy, who couldn't see, or talk, or hear at all by then. It was a sin my taking pleasure in that but I did, talking so sweetly to him in a loud voice and describing all the things he could no longer see and he couldn't tell me to be quiet or how he felt, just like when I was coming up and he never wanted to hear what I had to say. I'd learned to take vengeance gently, but it was a sin just the same.

"So I had gone home and was starting out again on my travels and enjoying the crisp early spring weather, and I see this body floating down river, dead as a doornail, and I don't even think, but wade right in there, fighting the current (I was strong back then) and saved the girl. It was a girl. I carried her dead body out of the river and prayed over her, and she come back to life, kinda rolls to the side and throws up all this water and some mud and coughs some and then lays back down and goes to sleep, but she was alive, I could feel her breathing. She had a cut on her neck, too, like someone had tried to cut her throat. Who'd do such a thing to a lovely young girl like that? Makes you wonder. But the river water was so cold it hadn't bled much and was already healing over. I searched in the wagon and found some disinfectant to put on it and that's all I ever did about that cut. She always had a scar there, but not that you'd notice when her hair hung down. It was a miracle, and I thanked God, but there was more to come, because God told me to believe what that girl said, for she came to speak the truth to me, and I would tell the truth to all the people who would listen. So I watched her while she slept and I noticed when she moved to curl up on her side that she was big with child, and when she woke up, I asked her who the father was, and she was all scared and could hardly speak, but she said, 'I ain't been with no one,' and then it hit me what God had been telling me. This humble girl was going to give birth to the Christ child all over again…this was it, the second coming we all been waiting for, and I believed it with all my heart. It still could be true. One thing I've learned is that if we don't acknowledge the miracles in our lives, they happen anyway and just get buried, as if they were nothing special with all the rest of our history. God knows how many miracles we've missed. Know what I mean, son?"

But the soldier had to go and the place was closing up for the night. JB looked so forlorn that he couldn't talk all night to the young man that the soldier and the owner both felt sorry for him and both gave him a few bucks, not knowing what else they could do for him, and he was too drunk by then to refuse and put the money in his briefcase with his plate and his Bible and the tabloids he liked to read in the morning with his coffee. "Guess I'll save this for a bus ticket to Florida," he said and stumbled up the street to the shelter.

The young man jogged home, hoping his mother would still be up, because he had to leave so early in the morning. Years later, she would always be thankful that she did get up before dawn to cook her son some eggs and watch him eat her food one last time, because it was not his destiny to return from the war. "Hey, Ma, you know that funny looking old man who sometimes preaches on the street corners, the one with the hat? I met him last night and he told me some stories about his life. Weird guy, and the funniest thing: he's only 42 years old."

"I don't believe it. That man looks to be 65 at least. That kind of life, I guess it ages folks. Poor man. I hope you gave him something."

"Sure, Ma, I did. You know, he said something interesting. He said Christ came back to earth in 1928, but no one noticed, or maybe something bad happened, I don't know, he didn't say, because it was closing time and we had to leave."

"There are too many crazies out there. I don't know whether to be afraid of them or afraid for them."

"Oh, Ma, this guy is harmless."

✢

When the young soldier went to the Greyhound station so early in the morning to catch his bus to Texas, there was a crowd in the alley and he asked what the commotion was about. "Some beggar fellow was killed last night over there." He hung around the edge of the crowd until the people dispersed a little and he saw that it was the preacher. He could hear the two cops talking, wondering why anyone would kill the guy, not like he had any money on him or anything, and the young man started to say that he did, that he'd given him $20 the night before, but he realized it would do no good, and maybe the cops would think he was involved, so he didn't say anything and went inside to wait for the bus. He was glad he'd talked his ma into kissing him good-bye at the house instead of coming down to the station with him. She'd have thought it was a bad omen for sure. He must have looked bad, thinking about the dead preacher, because the man he'd talked to outside came up and sat down right next to him and said, "What's the matter kid? You never saw a dead body before? Better get used to it, cuz where you're going, you'll see more than you can count." And then he laughed like he'd made some kind of joke and the soldier didn't know what to say, just excused himself and went to buy a newspaper and took it to another seat far away from the offensive laughing man.

When the cops searched JB's briefcase for clues, they found nothing helpful at all. There was his plate with a picture of Jesus on it and a Bible, that was to be expected, and a pile of old tabloids. It appeared that John the Baptist, as he was known to them, collected pictures of freaks. There were stories of two-headed children and children joined at the hip and an armless boy. The cops would have been more comfortable had the preacher collected girlie pictures, but this still gave no leads about the who, the why and the wherefore of the murder. Then the younger one noticed the handwriting in the margin of the paper about the boy with no arms. It was not easy to read the faded writing, but they persevered in their investigation.

"Beloved are we the sons of God, and it doth not yet appear what we shall be: but we know that, when He shall appear, we shall be like Him; for we shall see Him as He is. 1 John 3:2"

And then: "So Christ was once offered to bear the sins of many; and unto them that look for Him shall He appear the second time without sin unto salvation. Hebrews 9:28"

"So? Did this guy think that kid was the Christ come again?"

"Don't laugh. I remember this. He did, he gathered all kinds of people to follow him to some mountaintop where the mother, she was just a child herself, and this little girl gave birth to the kid with no arms. It was a terrible scandal because all these people had really believed him, that she was going to give birth to Christ all over again, that it was the second coming. He preached all over the state, dragging the poor girl around with him, and she was big as a whale."

"What? You followed him too?"

"I was only 12 at the time and staying with my grandparents while my dad looked for a job. They dragged me to these tent revivals all the time, so I was used to it, but this was different. I mean they were angry, you know, more disappointed than I'd ever seen them, and my grandparents had seen some rough times. They didn't take on so bad when they lost their farm. I don't know exactly what they expected as proof that this guy was for real, but they sure as hell didn't expect some deformed baby."

"They must have thought they'd lost their home in heaven too, I guess." And the older cop looked sad and whimsical at the same time, pondering what lengths folks would go to get a little comfort.

"Well it all worked out alright in the end. My dad got lucky, a job, and sent for all of us. They wouldn't let me tell him about us following that preacher around though, not ever, not 'til the day they died, first my granddad and then my grandma a few weeks later. They were just so embarrassed and ashamed to be taken in like that, and of course my dad never did buy any of that religious stuff…he'd've laughed them right out of the house if he knew."

"Did you ever tell him? I mean, after they died, did you?"

"No, never did, never told anyone until just now. Funny how things come 'round. Who'da thought I'd ever see this guy again? Poor fellow, I think he believed it and was as disappointed as the rest of them."

"What about the mother? She conscious during all this?"

"Hell, I think she still believed that kid was the Christ child, but then you know she was his mother, she loved him as if he were. Isn't that what mothers are supposed to do?"

"I don't think my ma was ever quite that fond of me. You?"

"She left us when I was little. That's why I was staying with the grand-parents."

"So much for what mothers are supposed to do, huh?"

"No sign of any kin? No one to notify, guess we should find a real preacher and see about burying him."

So John Banks, so miraculously born into this world, was buried in a pauper's grave at the wrong edge of town and forgotten by all but his Auntie Ada, who lived to be one hundred and one years old. The poor woman missed him and wondered about him all that long, long time, until a retired cop came to visit her after her picture was in a lot of newspapers with an interview to commemorate her 100th birthday, which coincided with the nation's bicentennial. That cop was no spring chicken himself by then, and they agreed there was one advantage to such a long life of toil and disappointments, and that was this: if you live long enough, you occasionally get to see some justice done, and after a while it don't seem like just an accident, because you get to glimpse a little piece of God's grand design. Anger and frustration and confusion do subside with time, and you get to know what peace feels like…if you live long enough.

VII

Auntie Ada, as she was know to just about everyone in the county, was 100 years old the year of the nation's bicentennial, just exactly half the age of the United States of America, so of course newspaper reporters came from all over the state and many parts of the country and just about interviewed her to death. Most of what she said they couldn't print, so most of them ended up enlarging her picture to take up more space and said a few words about all the events she had been a witness to during her century of life so far (even though she hadn't paid much attention to most of those events except the wars, being too preoccupied with the less momentous events of her own life). The lists were pretty much the same from one paper to the next, so her relatives did not bother saving but one or two of the articles for her scrapbook: war of course, presidential assassinations, the great depression and the civil rights movement, absolutely none of which she had ever approved of.

What Auntie Ada preferred to talk about were the difficulties she had encountered trying to raise her nephew John Banks, his penchant for preaching, his stubbornness, his days of glory, his downfall and then, finally, his disappearance. She would wonder out loud at least a dozen times a day if he were still alive, and if alive, where and how he was. Back in the sixties her stepchildren hired a private investigator to look for him just to get some peace, and when he could turn up nothing, he suggested they try the TV, but that proved useless as well. It irritated Auntie Ada no end that every week she had to watch long lost relatives reunite on television because some observant person out there in television land, as they called it, had been watching and called in with news of the lost folks, but no one ever called in about her John, whom she had loved in spite of all her scolding. "Was for his own good," she'd say over and over, but she could never rid herself of a private guilt and she'd been chewing on it for near half a century.

It was just about the time of the great depression she'd last seen him. She'd been so busy with him, she hadn't noticed she was getting on in years and hadn't thought about marriage or kids of her own until she was past bearing children. Then when it looked like she was in for a long life all alone, she was asked into holy matrimony by a widower with three children and she did care for them, somewhat more gently than she had cared for John. Her husband had passed on twenty years earlier at the ripe old age of 85, and being only five years his junior, she had thought to follow him soon thereafter, but her body just didn't seem to want to give up on her. Even one of her stepchildren passed before she did, and him the doctor in the family. Didn't seem right.

But reaching 100 was more laudable apparently than just lingering on into one's nineties, especially if the birthday coincided with the nation's bicentennial celebration. She didn't see what all the fuss was about and figured the reporters must be pretty hard up for news, and she'd tell them so right to their faces, and after a while, she just refused to do any more interviews. She'd pretend she wasn't home, hide in her bedroom with the lights off until they went away, like she was a criminal or owed someone money. It was damn irritating.

But then she got the letter. He was not a reporter, but a retired cop, who had seen her face in the paper, or maybe on the TV, yes that was it, praise be, the damn television came through at last. This cop had seen her on the television talking about her nephew John, and he said he thought he knew him and wanted to come talk to her. He didn't say what happened to the man he thought was her nephew, so she figured she'd better let him come to visit like he offered to do. He sent his phone number and told her it was okay to call collect, so she did as soon as she got his letter, and asked him right off the bat if he was working with some newspaper reporter, because she'd stopped talking to them, told him her lawyer told her not to talk to them, which was a lie, but Auntie Ada figured everyone else said it, why not her? She tried to ask him over the phone was her nephew alive and where, but he told her he wasn't sure the man he thought was her nephew might not be, so he'd rather come see her and ask some questions first.

So then he was there on her doorstep having driven the five hours from Charleston, and it occurred to him that the questions he needed to ask might be painful and the whole thing reminded him of when he was still in the force and had to visit families to ask questions about murder victims or murder suspects and how that was always, each and every time, right up to the very end, a problem for him.

After he'd partaken of the cookies and lemonade and candied watermelon rinds she offered him, he had to jump right in, there was no other way.

"The man I knew, in Charleston, well he'd been a preacher. And I know you mentioned that your nephew was a preacher and that he disappeared around 1930 or so. Can you tell me a little more? Was he the guy that claimed he had a woman with him was going to give birth to the second Christ?"

"You mean the second coming of Christ. There couldn't be a second Christ, you know."

"Well, yes, that. Was that your nephew?"

"Well, yes, kind of embarrassing actually. But, you know, a whole lot of folks fell for it. It didn't surprise me really, John pulling something like that. He always was a con man, but you know, I loved him anyway. The way you talk, I guess this guy you knew is dead?"

"He died a hero ma'am."

"Well, now I find that hard to believe. I loved him dearly, I just told you, and I did, but he never did fool me. He was a con man, plain and simple. Can you tell me where he died? And when? Had he ever married? Kids? Stuff like that? You know any of that about him? I don't need to hear about heroics."

But her caller looked so crestfallen that even outspoken Auntie Ada had to relent.

"Okay, I see I am a crotchety old woman. Here you want to cheer me up and tell me something fine about my own kin, and I'm telling you to put a lid on it. That's what the grandkids say to each other: 'put a lid on it.' No, you go ahead and tell me. What kind of hero was my John? Not a war hero, I know that, so don't go trying to tell me he was one of them."

"No ma'am, he wasn't a war hero, but he raised money for a shelter for homeless vets from the First World War, and he counseled young men going to the Second World War. Those of us who knew him on the street, that was his mission, you know, the street, nothing pompous or high and mighty about your John, no he was a humble man and those of us on the street admired that, that humility and that courage, because it takes courage, you know, to minister to the needs of the poor and the homeless…"

"What were you doing on the street back then? And when exactly was it? World War II, you say? You a cop then, or a soldier? Were you homeless?"

"No ma'am, I wasn't homeless, I was a cop back then. It was just after Pearl Harbor…"

"That when he died? Pearl Harbor? No wonder he never turned up when we went looking for him. He wasn't in trouble was he? I mean, you didn't have to arrest him, did you?"

"Oh, no ma'am, I didn't have to arrest him. He was a good man. He died saving a man." Now her visitor was thinking fast and making up a new story. He'd intended to tell her that her nephew had been killed in the war saving a fellow soldier, but she'd already warned him she wouldn't believe no war hero story, so he had to transfer the scene of his practiced monologue to the streets of Charleston.

"Stop right there, young man. If you're going to tell me my nephew John got involved in some other person's danger, we may as well say our good-byes, because it was another man you knew. My John avoided danger. I can believe he raised money for a shelter, especially if he was living there himself, and I can believe he talked the ears off any young man going off to war who would listen, but stopping someone else's bullet, no way, Jose, the grandkids always say that: 'no way, Jose,' and I know what they mean. No way. I knew my John."

"Well ma'am, I just wanted…"

"You just wanted to cheer me up, because you had to tell me my nephew was dead all these years and I didn't even know it. But you can't and you don't have to. I got worse to worry about than whether John died an ordinary man or a hero. I got my own conscience to worry about, is the fact of the matter. You see, I never said good-bye to him the last time he left home. You don't know where he is buried do you? Do you think an old woman like me could make the trip? I sure would love to lay a few daisies on his grave, say a proper good-bye."

"I'm not sure, ma'am, it was a long time ago. I could try to find the grave, I guess. I could drive you back with me to Charleston, and you could take the bus back home. Would you want to do that? I can't guarantee I can find the grave after all these years, but I'd be willing to try."

"You're the hero, young man. Did you know that?" and Auntie Ada smiled at him almost flirtatiously.

"Well we can't leave now if it's all the way back to Charleston and it wouldn't do for me to have a man under my roof. I'll call a few friends and see if we can't get you put up for the night. That okay with you? I have a stepson who has a guest room, now his son is off to college. What do you think? But he's a ways over the mountain. I'm trying to think if one of the old geezers here in town has an extra room. You got to call your wife or anything?"

"My wife's dead, ma'am, and I live alone now, but thank you. I'll be okay at the Motel 6 right outside town. I'll pick you up in the morning. What time can you be ready to travel?"

"Well now, hold on a minute. I'll get you some dinner first. Then we'll make plans for the morning. I should warn you I'm old and slow and probably won't be ready to leave until nearly 9 o'clock."

And that was how Auntie Ada made a new friend who was willing to listen to her stories about the old days, and could be trusted not to tell the papers or any of her neighbors, either.

It was a beautiful day for driving, and seeing the landscape pass by reminded Auntie Ada of things she'd long forgotten. She recalled how, after John had gone traveling, a man that had been gone for years and gone to war too, had returned to the county with a beautiful wife and what a sad story that had been. "Killed her in the end…it was the talk of the county for a couple of years, poor man, she'd been fooling around on him, right under his nose, folks said. No one blamed him, but you know he blamed himself. Was never the same after that. I'll never forget that look he had in his eyes, and yet, here I go rambling on and on, and I did forget all about it until just now."

"I gather he didn't go to jail? Maybe he'd have felt better if he had."

"Oh, no, I don't think so. I know what you mean, but he was a strange fellow, half Indian, I heard."

"You think Indians are strange? What if I was to tell you I was half Indian? What would you think then?"

"Oh mercy me, are you? Are you really?"

"No, but what if I was to tell you that?"

"Well what are you then? So's I don't go embarrassing myself again."

"Italian. That okay?"

"Of course it is. You know I don't mean nothing by that kind of talk. We all just talk that way, you know, about folks as are different. And we always heard stories about Indian magic, like that they could turn themselves into animals like that, so you know, people were just a little bit afraid of Indians when I was coming up, and we all get our ideas when we're young, don't you think?"

"Well I hope we get a few ideas when we get old, too. So, did you know that there was a time when folks thought old women were witches?"

"What? You trying to get me mad?"

"No, I just thought you'd think that was an interesting idea. I mean, you and I know that old women are not witches. Why, we even know there's no such thing as witches, but a hundred years ago, some folks thought there were witches and that old women could work some bad magic. Sometimes folks would burn or drown an old woman just because it was so strange for a woman to live so long, know what I mean?"

"You are trying to get me mad. Did you say you were a retired cop? Or a school teacher?"

"My wife was a school teacher. I was the cop."

"I see." And then Auntie Ada was quiet for a while, wondering who it was used to burn old women just for being old, and just exactly what this guy was up to, now he had her prisoner in his car all the way to Charleston.

"Funny how things change over time though, ain't it? Nowadays no man would kill his wife for committing adultery. Why, we have these young people coming in to buy land and they build themselves some cabins and call themselves a 'commune,' and I heard they all sleep together or take turns with the husbands and wives, something like that, and no one kills anybody else. In fact they make a big deal about being against war and hunting and what not."

"Yeah, we got some newcomers to the counties around Charleston, too. Nice young folks mostly. Think?"

"Well sure. I don't understand 'em but I'm glad they don't go killing each other over some silly jealousy. I never did understand it but maybe that's because I didn't get married myself 'til I was already past 40, regular old maid I was. No one thought I was much to look at, but now we all look alike anyway; the men, the women, you get to be 100 and what difference does it make, huh? I felt sorry for that pretty woman, being pretty just got her dead. And you know, it's a small world, because it was her daughter what had the baby my John told everyone was the second coming of the Christ, God knows what got into him. He couldn't have been in love with her, she was but 14 at the time, 13, 14, something like that. She just didn't want to tell who got her pregnant. Some folks kept pretty busy wondering what boy did it. I don't think John did it, pretty sure he didn't. John wanted people's admiration and sometimes their money, but he wouldn't have done that to a young girl like that. Said he fished her out the river. And her poor father, no one ever could find him after that. They was other sad stories too, from the old days. Want to hear 'em?"

"Why didn't you tell the papers?"

"Oh, they don't want to hear what I got to say. They already know what they want to put in their stories, and if you tell them what they want to hear, they quote you on it, and if you tell them something else, they still quote you saying what they wanted you to say, know what I mean? I mean all them lawyers telling folks not to talk to the papers is right, I think."

So Auntie Ada rambled on, barely stopping for breath, because most young folks thought the old ones were boring and never had a naughty thought in their lives, but she knew different. She told about the old couple that ran the general store right up into their eighties, and how that little old woman was one of the best bear hunters in the county because, way back before anyone could remember, her husband had left her alone on the farm with the young farmhand, while he went to hunt bear for a couple of weeks, and when he came home, he found her in the hayloft with the farmhand, and he shot the farmhand, but he didn't shoot his wife. He just took her with him next time he went bear hunting. But small world that it was, it was their grandson, Ada was pretty sure, who'd been caught with the pretty woman in the shed, and the husband had shot them both that time. Well, for all the self-righteous gossips might like to point the finger, it happened all the time, then as now, except now people were out in the open about it and got a divorce instead of killing each other.

"Not always," thought the cop. The fact was, nothing ever really changed much about human beings, but the clothing styles

They stopped to eat in Hinton and were hungry again by the time they got to Charleston, and Auntie Ada was getting tired from the drive and ended up staying the night with the cop's sister. And the next day the three of them went searching among the remains of the paupers' cemetery that had once been at the edge of town and was now surrounded by new buildings and neighborhoods, and the subject of some controversy as to whether it should be turned into a parking lot. No one mentioned any of that to Auntie Ada, and finally they did find the grave that was marked "JB," and Auntie Ada said a prayer and laid down the store-boughten flowers she had gotten for the occasion that morning, and then she was ready to go home, to lay down her guilt and her questions and go about her business as she had always tried to do; a no-nonsense kind of woman, they called her (and if that was so, some wondered, how is it that John turned out to be so full of it?).

But then a funny thing happened. Auntie Ada was too tired to take the bus home that afternoon, and she was welcome to stay another night with the sister, so she did, and the poor woman came in the next morning to find that Auntie Ada had died quietly, and presumably comfortably, in her sleep. "She just wanted to find out what happened to her nephew," she told her brother, and he just sighed and said he was going to write a book.

Discreet as they tried to be, they had to contact he woman's stepchildren about the death and make arrangements to transport the body back to Greenbriar County, and so the local newspapers did get hold of the story after all, at least that part of it that they wanted to tell. And wouldn't you know? One of them reporters did some research in old newspaper archives and dug up the stories about the baby born with no arms and hounded the retired cop until he told his part of it, what he knew, which was more than they had expected, but he didn't know that, all of which just goes to show that Auntie Ada was right about not talking to the reporters. It all made pretty interesting reading that year.

And then a folksinger made up a song and sang it at the state fair in Lewisburgh, and every now and then, someone up and claimed to BE the baby boy, James, who'd been lost track of during the great depression, never mind that he'd be 47 by now, and was born with no arms, or even that he was a he. It was a sin for folks not to believe in the death and resurrection. It was a sin for folks not to believe in the virgin birth some nearly 2,000 years ago, so why shouldn't folks be asked to believe that Christ had returned in the form of a baby James, who could stay forever young, grow him a pair of arms, or even change himself into a young woman? The thing was, the mental hospitals were running out of room and money and letting folks out that shouldn't have been let out, and soon they were all wandering the streets and preaching and claiming to be someone else. And when the newspaper stories hit the stands, those folks just had something new to hope for, some new escape route from the reality that had driven them crazy in the first place. That was one theory. And then there were those who thought maybe it could be true, why not? And then there were those who always responded the same way to every new thing that came up: "What is this world coming to?" Which was a damn silly question when you thought about it, the world had been coming to something for so long and nobody seemed to ever get it figured out. And that was how the talk went on the streets, until the stories died down, when something new came along to catch the interest of the reporters.

But that retired cop, maybe because he'd actually seen them, the mother and the baby, when he was a young motherless child himself, or maybe just because he'd been a cop all those years and got used to wondering about such things, did indeed drive himself nearly crazy trying to track them down. That investigation occupied him for the rest of his life and led him on many false paths, but not so false, maybe because he met a lot of sorry folks who were cheered by his interest in their stories, even when the stories turned out to be the wrong ones. His sister once scolded him about the amount of time and money he put into the search, but when he asked her what else he had to spend his time and money on, she couldn't come up with anything, so she stopped scolding. She'd been old enough to go work for a family while her younger brother was being dragged around the countryside by their lunatic grandparents to tent revivals and getting all worked up over religious prophecies. She married a nice man who made a good living, and they had raised two fine children, and she'd earned some peace and quiet, so she was off to her bridge game and her brother could do whatever he damn well pleased.

✢

Last night I dreamt
you came to me
caressed my hair
stroked my cheek
stop my tears
so I can sleep.

But then I woke
to find you gone
and I was left
to know alone
alone I was
left to know

I'd always be

Where did you go?
Why did you go?
Taking with you
all the joy
I'd ever know?

"All these years I've tracked them, the mother Mary and her baby James, and then last night I remembered where I had seen her last and it was enough that I had. When the singer at the concert had thrummed her last wounding chord, I was crying, because the scene came back to me with that sound, that sad, mournful guitar sound. It was at a carnival at the state fair after Dad got work and we had moved to Charleston, but before my grandparents died. I saw her there, playing the guitar on a stage with some other women, guitars and fiddles and banjos, and the music was merry, not sad, merry for dancing, but that one woman, still just a girl, she had a look in her eye that was shiny with the unshed tears of a hundred sad souls. She played a solo while I watched and sang a ballad, and then she thrummed that sad guitar and the whole story was laid before me in a flash, the sadness of it, the sadness of being human in this world. I didn't know her story, but I knew her story was sad."

Part III

Mary Queen of Scots

VIII

The house was less than modest, small and shabby in fact and in a rough neighborhood, but Rose of Sharon had created a real rose garden in the tiny yard, a garden in which to thrive in her own unique and mysterious way. Her father, a Baptist preacher, had succumbed to the despair that he inherited from generations of suicides and petty criminals with big dreams. He looked back on this heritage of failure and, considering his own life, decided God didn't care for him and life was hopeless. Rose of Sharon, so named by her father during his years of religious zealotry, found him hanging one afternoon and arranged for the burial and her own independent life with a noticeable lack of emotion, thus earning for herself a reputation for being mentally deficient and deranged. She didn't care because this reputation ensured her privacy and independence; things she had longed for during all the years of her father's supervision.

Her father had owned the little house passed to him by his mother and so Rose or Sharon, as she sometimes called herself one name and sometimes the other, did not have to worry about a place to live. She did have to think, however, about where to get money for food and clothes and coal in the winter. But first she wanted to dance, and the first thing she did when she realized she could do anything she wanted was to go where the soldiers went to dance.

Sharon, which was the name she used when out dancing, had always yearned to dance, and there had been the young men who came calling and invited her to dances, but her father forbade it, believing it to be sinful in itself and certainly a precursor to fornication, as he so often admonished her. And Rose, as she called herself at home, did as she was told.

So now Sharon danced every night, flirting with the soldiers on the way to the war in Europe. She loved it when they fell in love with her and bought her pretty dresses and took her out to dinner in restaurants. She believed she was entitled finally to this life of glamour. She cut and curled her hair and painted her face and began to collect beaux, who sometimes fought over her, which she very much enjoyed.

Even when she was home alone, doing mundane things like stripping the peas from the pods that grew in the backyard garden, or washing her stockings, she would be self-conscious and move with a certain provocative grace, as if one of her young men were spying on her. It was one of her fantasies. Climbing the ladder in the kitchen to reach for canned goods stored on the highest shelf, she imagined herself lifted down in strong arms and kissed tenderly on the lips. Being so romantic, her first actual sexual experience was disappointing, but it had taken place in the dark, and she was glad he couldn't see her face as she mouthed words of everlasting love, for he was quite ecstatic and proposed marriage on the spot. Sharon wasn't sure she wanted to give up all the others and her chances for something better, but she was afraid she might become pregnant and then would want to make sure he did marry her, so she said her mother had always told her to think about such a serious step and not rush into something so sanctified and permanent as marriage in the first flush of passionate love. Sharon's mother had run away with another man when her father began preaching, and she only vaguely remembered her, but Sharon read a lot of books and knew how to talk well. Then she asked if he would buy her an engagement ring and they could plan their wedding more carefully.

By the time the young man, no older than Sharon in fact, was to be sent overseas, Sharon knew she was not pregnant, and she sent him off to war with kisses and sweet words and no intention whatsoever to wait for him as she promised. She had by then, also learned how to prevent such accidents as pregnancy or disease and was more careful with subsequent lovers. To some she introduced herself as Rose, sensing their need for a quiet, homebody kind of girl, and to others she introduced herself as Sharon, seeing that they were looking for a girl who knew how to enjoy herself. She never went with more than two men at a time, and it pleased her to think of her lovers meeting somewhere and discussing their respective sweethearts without ever knowing that Rose and Sharon were one and the same. She avoided conflicts by feigning illness or becoming temporarily upset over some imagined transgression, making her beau pay with guilt and remorse and a gift of some kind before she'd welcome him back into her arms. Since all of these young men were in Newport News on their way across the sea, Sharon, or Rose, as the mood might take her, was continually saying good-bye, usually with some relief, either because she didn't love the fellow, or sensed that he didn't really love her.

Then, as suddenly as she had begun her life of glamour and romance, Rose of Sharon tired of it, became depressed and decided she wanted someone older, stronger, richer, who would take care of her and not leave her ever. She was almost afraid to find him too soon and well she might have been, for she did find the man of her dreams and he did love her for a while only to finally tell her that he was married and couldn't possibly marry her and gave her money to abort the child she carried. That was when she became a recluse in her garden and found a job waitressing and avoided men altogether.

And it was shortly thereafter that a dark and brooding man, always alone, almost handsome in an odd sort of way, began to come daily into the diner where she worked. He spoke with a slight accent, Scottish, he told her, along with other things, like being the son of the son of a duke from Edinburgh and wanting to go back to claim the family estate from the thieving Englishmen who had driven his family out and to America. That was Charles' fantasy, based on putting two and two together when he listened to his father's cryptic stories of his past. Charles had signed up with the army expecting to make it to Scotland where he would research his family history and perhaps find a life for himself there. He had wandered all over this country and was older than the young soldiers Rose of Sharon was used to, but different as well, from the older married man who had so cruelly deceived her. She approached Charles carefully, waiting on him every day and asking him more and more questions, while avoiding answering the questions he put to her.

Charles was so shy that it was Rose who finally asked him to go out dancing one evening, but Charles couldn't dance, and she ended up taking him home. To her astonishment, Charles, a good ten years older than she, was a virgin, and he explained, with some embarrassment that she found endearing, that he had been waiting for the right woman. So Rose of Sharon, who had been so devastated by her last experience with an older man, began to feel powerful again. She would learn later that his need was more powerful still.

Then the day came when Rose of Sharon dressed very carefully, examined her lovely face in the mirror time and time again and waited for Charles with a traumatizing mix of excitement and anxiety, for she was, once again, pregnant. She had expected to entice him into marriage with her beauty and sweet, well-rehearsed words, but in fact, when he finally arrived with the news he was being sent to France, she just threw up. Charles held her head, gently stroking back her hair while she vomited into the flower garden, bathed her face and said sweet words to her. When she was finally able to choke out the words that she was pregnant, he kissed her and told her that they would get married quickly before he left and then have a real wedding when he returned. She was so relieved that it never occurred to her to remember that he hadn't really asked her. Where she had once been jealous of her freedom to choose, now she felt too helpless to assert it.

Finding the ring, the JP and a special dress for the sad little ceremony kept her busy, and the whole thing happened so quickly that neither she nor Charles felt the full impact. In fact, the marriage changed his life forever, but changed hers hardly at all. Rose of Sharon had a destiny that she moved toward in spurts and starts, but it didn't matter much who would be the facilitator of that destiny. But for Charles, Rose of Sharon was his destiny; it would be she who bestowed his greatest joy and she who would be the death of him.

Sanchez

She saw Charles off as she had seen off so many young men and, as was her pattern, she went dancing. Leaving the wedding ring in a carved wood box on her dresser and hiding her thickening condition inside a corset, Rose of Sharon cut and curled her hair and painted her face and collected beaux as she once had, secure in the knowledge that when she needed him, Charles would be back to take care of her and their little daughter. She knew she was going to have a girl child, because she dreamed of her almost every night, and she had already chosen the name: Mary Queen of Scots.

Although she danced and teased, Rose of Sharon had become quite chaste, which caused some of her dance partners to get quite angry. She took this anger as a tribute to her desirability and her power and was most exhilarated when she danced on the edge of danger. An older woman, an unabashed prostitute, whom Sharon had seen around, warned her once that she would come to no good end, but Sharon only laughed at her. She was always Sharon now when she went out, being Rose to Charles, who expressed a particular fondness for that name, and called her the most beautiful rose in the garden, a quaint compliment that touched her with its innocence, herself being, by now, so sophisticated.

Then came a time she could no longer hide her condition, and she disappeared from the night spots and stayed in her garden through the winter and the spring, dancing by herself to music on the radio. One spurned suitor who had followed her for some time found her and found out that she was married and in a rage threatened to come back when her husband returned from the war and tell the poor man what his wife had been up to while he risked his life for his country and cursed her to an eternity in hell for what she had done to two upstanding soldiers.

Much as it pained her to think of leaving her garden, she wrote to Charles suggesting that when he was done with war (not when the war was over, but when *he* was done with it, like it was his choice) that they settle in Scotland, and she told him then of her intention to name their child Mary Queen of Scots, and what did he think of that? It was months before she received and answer and lucky, she thought, to receive it at all. Charles was happy with the name, asked how she knew it would be a girl and what she would name a son, suggesting Jamie might be a good name for a boy. He didn't discuss the idea of settling in Scotland, but told her he looked forward to going back to his old home place in West Virginia after the war, a thought that quite appalled Rose, but she knew that they would have to go somewhere to avoid the risk of being confronted with old suitors, or neighbors with gossip.

Charles didn't make it home in time for the birth of their child, or her first birthday, or her second birthday. A neighbor lady, who Rose thought disliked

76

her, surprised Rose by assisting her at the birth, which came on sudden and a little early. Rose, a healthy girl, if a bit too slender, was up and about sooner than she expected and ready to dance again. Ida, the neighbor lady, old enough to be the child's grandmother or even great grandmother, found herself very attached to the exquisite little Mary Queen of Scots (odd name, thought Ida), which was lucky for both of them, as Sharon imposed shamelessly on Ida's kindness and left the baby with her many nights, while she resumed her life of glamour, music and flirtation.

Not long after, Sharon returned home in the dark of night, hiding bruises on her face and arms, where the infuriated suitor of her past had beaten her when he found her dancing with one of his buddies. He had called her all kinds of cruel names and the memory of those names stung her more than the bruises. In the morning she covered her face with make-up that barely disguised the black and blue marks and wore a long-sleeved dress when she went to retrieve Mary from Ida's house. Ida could see plainly what had happened and tried to offer comfort to Rose, one woman to another, but Rose was proud and took Mary home without so much as a thank you and that was the last time for a long time that Ida had the child to herself overnight. It was sad for Mary, who missed the good woman and the nurturance she had enjoyed. But soon she would be walking and would find her own way to her granny's garden, where she spoke her first words and spent many happy hours, while her mother slept the days away in a quiet despair. Rose could not understand why Sharon kept getting her into trouble, but she was resigned to staying home, being careful and waiting for Charles. She began to pour her periodic waves of energy into long letters, which she would add to day by day, until after a few weeks, she would mail the veritable package to Charles, who would receive it months later. Charles took courage from being so much loved and in fact was a distinguished soldier who won more than one medal for bravery. He began to feel invincible and took chances and miraculously never pushed his luck to the limit, for he arrived home at the end of the war without a scratch.

Rose, meantime, had settled into the image of a tragic heroine, a princess trapped in a tower and the tower was her own depression, which alternated with euphoria, but lasted longer and longer as she languished in the garden, letting the weeds take over, ignoring the bounty of the sweet pea vines and the berry bushes. Not wanting them to go to waste, Ida came over and she and Mary, now well past two, shelled them into a large cooking pot (but eating most of them raw as they worked). Rose allowed Ida to take over without a word of protest or gratitude, just watching them, the old woman and the child, with a certain remote curiosity, as if they were strangers. "It happens sometimes," Ida explained to her old husband and concentrated on loving the bright and beautiful little girl, Mary Queen of Scots: odd name, everyone said.

Often Rose would cry like an abandoned child, and she didn't understand the source of her tears. When Charles came home she broke into tears then too, and he thought they were tears of joy, and Rose didn't know what they were but sobbed for hours in his arms, while he soothed her, stroking her hair, kissing the top of her head. They didn't go get Mary at Ida's house until the morning, Charles euphoric from the night, Rose still sleepy and lethargic. She watched him in that detached way she had, while he looked at his daughter for the first time and kneeled down to embrace her and explain to her who he was. He had thought Rose would have prepared the child, but of course she had not, and it was Ida and her husband who cajoled Mary into giving a proper greeting to her father, and explained to him how little children were. He thanked them for helping his wife care for his daughter while he was away, and it was clear to everyone that now he would take over and be the head of the family and that he planned to move away. It was a sad day for Mary, Ida and even Ida's husband when the little family sold Rose of Sharon's tiny house and set out by wagon for West Virginia. Ida embraced the little girl and promised to see her soon, but knew better than to ask them to write or keep in touch. "Odd folks," she thought out loud when she could no longer see them on the road. "Odd folks," her husband agreed. They both left unspoken their fears for the child.

Charles had saved most of his pay (sending some back to Rose) to buy another cabin on another piece of land that lay near his old home. He carried Mary on his shoulders, and Rose followed him as he showed them the creeks, the hills, the great oaks, the tight hollers and many paths worn by the predictable journeys of deer looking for food. Some thought the dense forest spooky, but Rose and Charles and Mary, each in their own way and separately, all loved it, and found refuge in it. Sometimes Charles went back to the graves of his parents but he never took Rose or told her anything about them. The first time he felt angry at Rose, angry enough to want to strike her, he remembered the frightening fury of his father and the pain he had felt when his mother was hurt and he did not, then or ever, lay a hand on his beloved wife. He ran into the forest for hours and did not come home until well after dark, and Rose was frightened to be left alone in the vast and isolated woods and didn't know if or when her husband would return. She had cried herself to sleep before he came home and he lay down beside her quietly, not wanting to wake her, preferring to watch her and ponder her mystery.

They soon acquired a cow for milk and chickens and some goats and geese, who simply settled on a widening of the creek they called a pond. Mary spent most of her time with these animals, getting so little attention from either of her parents. If she wandered off just beyond their view, they would both panic and run about calling her name, and she'd let them do that for a while before showing herself and letting them hug and cuddle her and cry with relief. In this manner, Mary assured herself that her mother and father did indeed love her. On holiday occasions other folks in the county came to visit and to welcome Charles home after all those years he was away, but Rose did not like the plain and hardworking people. She did enjoy the dances, though, and danced with all the men, old and ugly as some of them were, and all the men enjoyed dancing with such a graceful and vivacious young woman. In this manner, Rose isolated herself among the women who were her neighbors. Charles didn't see it and Charles couldn't see it, being so proud that his wife was the prettiest, the liveliest wherever they went.

But at home Rose was morose and the forest suited her mood perfectly, hiding her, enfolding her in a permanent twilight. Only occasionally did she seek the sun, aware of its warmth on her arms like the sensual stroke of a lover, some imagined lover, that watched her from the woods and would show himself one day. She knew that Charles was a good man and loved her and she loved him too in her own peculiar way, but Rose yearned for adventure and even tragedy, tragedy being a kind of adventure. To Rose of Sharon, life was not sacred, but an experiment and more and more often and for longer periods, a burden, and she searched for someone to commit her suicide, grandly, with poignancy and drama. She yearned for the man who would die for love as she herself wanted to do, for love was like the butterflies, so briefly glorious. It seemed a sacrilege to let it simply wither and dry out and linger like that forever, for to Rose it was beauty and drama that were sacred.

Imagining scenes of passion and tenderness, Rose of Sharon stood one evening in the garden where she had been picking the first tomatoes for the evening meal and felt the breeze blow her skirt around her legs and watched the leaves of the trees flutter like her skirt and show their silver undersides in anticipation of the coming storm, and she felt the rain-laden wind on her cheek, and she cried and cried, knowing she wanted to be pure poetry, wanted to fly and drift with the clouds and yet, there she stood with a basket of tomatoes on her arm and a child and husband inside the too-warm house waiting for their meal. Innocent and loving they were, and Rose of Sharon felt sorry for them and for herself and for all who lived chained to the earth and tantalized by its visions of beauty just beyond their reach, in the sky, in the wind, in the water, in the caves and in the very heart of multi-colored rocks that erupted from the very heart of the earth itself. If she could have said these things to Charles, they would have found their common bond and mutual sympathy. But Rose of Sharon rarely spoke to Charles except to ask or answer questions about purely practical matters, and her lovemaking had become remote and distant and puzzling to him.

As Mary got older and sturdier, Charles spent more and more time with her, taking her with him when he wandered through the woods and teaching her the names and uses of plants and trees. They got the wood in together in the fall, enough to last the winter. And they dug the sassafras roots that laced through the earth, not deep, but long, so they had to work for hours to get it all, and then they peeled off bits of the red bark and tasted it right there with the taste of the earth still on it. Then they brought it to Rose, who washed it and scraped it and made them a drink sweetened with honey. They gathered the wild mint together and the winterberries and the blackberries that grew in a thorny tangle wherever the trees allowed the sun to penetrate, and the blueberries that grew on top of the little mountain beyond their home, so steep that when they climbed it, they had to reach for the roots of trees to pull themselves up until they reached the flat, rocky top, where huge birds nested and screamed at them when they came too close.

Mary became accustomed to the silences of her parents, for neither had the energy to talk about the mundane, and both protected their wild fancies from the scrutiny of more practical people. As a child, curious about everything, she frustrated both of them with her continual questions and interruptions, and so each had taken to preoccupied silence in her presence. Sometimes they talked to each other in the night in whispers, in the frenzy of passion or the tenderness of satiation, usually when the storms came and the wind blew the house so Mary worried it might blow apart and send them all flying, and lightening cut the sky like a sudden dagger. Storms always awakened her mother's energy, her love, her passion, but Mary was more afraid of those sudden outbursts than she was hurt by the more usual inattentiveness. She already knew that her mother lived in another world, and Mary made her own world, her own life. It was Charles she loved, who taught her to read and add numbers and took her with him everywhere, to the livestock auction, to the bank in the nearest town, to the dry goods store. Mary went with him when he bought the lovely lavender satin and lace for Rose to sew into a wedding gown, for they had never yet had their real wedding like he promised.

They had their wedding party outside on an early autumn day beneath the bright blue sky, cloudless, and the warm sun made Rose feel faint in her satin. A minister from the town came out to preside over the ceremony, and everyone was solicitous of Rose for Charles's sake. Charles had brought her a peacock and a peahen as wedding gifts, and they screeched and screamed on the porch. The brilliant male was molting and left feathers like jewels in the mud around the barnyard, and Mary ran around collecting them with delight. When he was naked, the peacock became quiet at last. "Embarrassed," Mary thought, and her mother agreed with her, smiling on her and blessing the occasion.

IX

Mary was six when her parents had their wedding, and when she realized that she had been unhappy, for she realized that now she hoped that things would be different. Rose of Sharon rewarded Charles for his gesture with a great deal of tenderness, even cheerfulness and talked fast and excited to Mary and Charles about the birds, the garden, the weather, the woods. She began to make friends with the women of the county, who grudgingly forgave her her beauty that never seemed to fade, not with work or sun or wind. She took pleasure in milking the cow and gathering the eggs and picking the wild berries with her daughter and husband. She even read to them at night by the fire, fairy tales mostly, from books that had belonged to Charles's father, fairy tales from Scotland and Ireland as well as history books, but Rose ignored the serious histories, preferring the aura of an even older antiquity in the tales.

Some nights Mary had nightmares about the stories, and her mother was by her side the instant she began to cry, comforting her and hearing the story of the bad dream and telling her it was only a dream. Some nights Mary was afraid to go to sleep, afraid to dream, but then she braved it, knowing her mother would be there if she woke up crying. Mary would always remember that winter as a kind of tapestry filled with the characters of the stories and her dreams and intimate moments in the dark with her mother and her father, who always followed, sleepy and sweet to her bedside. And filled, too, with the fragrances of cooking with her mother, standing on a stool to reach the table to roll out the dough for strudel and sniffing the cinnamon, learning to knead the bread dough, redolent with the sweet strange smell of the yeast, secretly tasting on her finger the apple wine brewing near the wood stove. And filled with the colors and patterns of the fabrics her mother sewed into dresses for her, always with a ruffle around the hem. And the button- eyed face of the rag doll her mother made with the remnants, the doll she dressed like her daughter, and Mary loved the doll until she left it one day by accident in the barnyard, running from a rooster gone crazy when she went alone to collect the eggs, and her mother found the doll in the mud and screamed and cried as if the doll were her own child, and ever after, that button-eyed face appeared in dreams as a demon to frighten Mary, and Mary couldn't tell her mother she woke crying from a dream about the doll, somehow she knew she couldn't tell her that.

With the spring came a madness so clear that Charles took Rose away to a hospital in a town almost all the way to Roanoke and he didn't bring her home for weeks. When he did, Rose of Sharon was silent and seemed tired all the time. Slowly she found her strength and her energy and by summer, was lively again and ready to dance. Her husband was grateful then and so was her daughter, and Charles and Mary thought, in the simplicity of relief, that all was well forever.

On the Fourth of July they went to the dance in the town, the town being by then a post office, a general store, a sawmill and some houses. The dance was in a large open room on the second floor of the building that housed the post office. There was an old man, who played fiddle, and his son, who played the banjo, and a caller for the square dances. Mary sat and watched during the intricate square dances, but in between those, were the other dances where old grannies danced with each other and parents danced with toddlers and some folks even danced alone, doing some fancy footwork to impress the crowd. Rose of Sharon twirled Mary around in a dance, the picture of lovely young motherhood, and a young man back home to visit his grandparents watched them and felt his heart wrap around her whirling form, like a string around a top. That night everyone danced with everyone else and it was okay for the young Duane to ask Rose to dance while Charles danced one with Mary. It was a waltz and they talked some. Neither one of them ever took their eyes from the other's, and it was a miracle they didn't dance into people, but they waltzed around the room perfectly, as though they had been dancing together forever. Some folks noticed, but Charles was busy with Mary and happy and breathless when he got his wife for the next square dance. Duane sat out the rest of the evening, watching Rose thread through the room, the room itself and everyone in it touched with an aura of magic for the young man due to leave the next day.

But Duane couldn't bear the thought of leaving even though he knew that Rose was married and a mother, and he stayed and got a job at the sawmill and lived with his grandparents, who were glad to have him. They ran the general store even into their eighties, and soon Duane convinced his grandmother to retire and stay home and bake and he would stand behind the counter now, having left the sawmill job, and wait for Rose of Sharon to come in to buy some calico and coffee and yeast and candy. She did love candy. Usually it was Charles who had come into town to do their business, but he was encouraged now that Rose had the energy to come with him, and while he negotiated for seasoned lumber, she could mull over the fabrics for Mary's new dress. Sometimes Mary went with her father, sometimes with her mother, and Mary didn't like the way the young shopkeeper talked to her mother, and she asked a lot of questions that her mother didn't answer. "He's just nice is all," she'd tell Mary and give her daughter a piece of the hard candy. "You want the red one?" she'd ask, and Mary would nod yes, not really caring and worrying, always worrying.

Duane suggested to his granny that she revive the old sewing bees she used to have at her house. It turned out to be a good idea and a few women were delighted to come in once a week and talk and sew, and he told Rose about it, and she surprised all the women by coming a couple of times. But they weren't surprised when she stopped. After the first couple of weeks, she went straight to the store, which Duane closed for lunch, and they made love in the back storeroom on a bed he made of sacks of beans and rice and covered with his coat. She was only a few years older than he was, but her motherhood made her seem a goddess to him, and he could hardly contain his joy that she would deign to take him as her lover. But then he wanted more and he began to plan a way to have her all the time, thinking that was what she wanted, too. He started making trips to Roanoke and Covington, looking for a job that would pay him enough to rent a house for the two of them, then he thought they should go further, all the way to New York perhaps, or out west, somewhere nobody could ever find them. He didn't tell Rose because he didn't want to get her hopes up, so he just looked and planned and waited to tell her the good news when the good news was certain. She complained sometimes about his frequent trips and laughed that she had to actually go and sew with his grandmother and think of things to tell the ladies there, because if she stopped going once a week into town alone, Charles would wonder and ask questions. Duane felt a twinge of discomfort that she was so adept at deception, but he attributed it to the great love they shared, and he thought about all the deceptive things he had had to do and say to get them even this little time together, and he thought about his plans and was proud of his self-control in not telling Rose anything until he could surprise her with a perfectly laid plan: the city, the job and the house all arranged for. He was too young and selfish to even think about Mary. And when he occasionally did think about Mary, he reasoned that she seemed to prefer her father anyway, and that there were plenty of women in the county who would jump at the chance to marry Charles and be a mother to his daughter. It helped to think of Mary as Charles's daughter; he hated to think of Rose being with Charles, having carried his child, so Duane didn't think that far back.

So went the fall and then the first snows came and it was a long and cold winter, so the snow never completely melted before another blanket of it fell over the town and the hills and homesteads. Charles always came into town with Rose now the winter had come and they came into town very seldom. Duane felt like he was dying a slow death, and once Rose found herself alone with him and told him to be patient and they would meet again in the spring, in the woods, in a special spot she had found, a magical place, she told him, and she seduced him with words all over again, and her words, rehearsed like a prayer every night, helped him get through the winter; her words and his plans.

Sometimes Charles came into the store alone and sometimes he talked to Duane one man to another, never dreaming Duane's secret. He thought Duane was simply shy like he was, and he liked him. In fact, the two men were very much alike in many ways, but neither knew this for sure. They talked about the war, and finally Duane began to ask questions and became somewhat animated, speculating on the excitement of battle. He had been a child during the war and was bitter that he would never have his chance to distinguish himself.

"I wouldn't worry. I was thirty when I went. But you really shouldn't be hoping for another war. You think it is exciting because all us old soldiers come in and talk about our own best moments, when we were brave and saved ourselves and our friends and our country. We talk like that because we are too ashamed to tell the truth about it."

"I don't understand what you mean."

"I mean, and you don't have to be repeating this to your granddad, I mean that it's all we could do to save ourselves, and more often than not, we watched companions die because there wasn't anything we could do to save them, sometimes, by accident, we could do that, do some act of bravery, but you know that bravery means you think about what you are doing. We didn't have time to think about anything. This wasn't a war like the old wars, this was worse. All kinds of modern weapons, like the magic tricks of the devil was what this was. I got all those medals and I don't remember even once feeling brave. For me the most excitement was when I got letters from my wife, and it was those letters got me through alive, and they had their own magic, those letters."

Duane fell silent then, but Charles had tapped memories that kept flooding his brain, and he liked this young man and he talked on most of the afternoon, sitting by the wood stove, and no one came into the store because a storm was whipping up, and Charles himself should have been on his way. All Duane remembered later of that day was a story about a soldier leaving for home and being caught with an arm in his duffle bag; a souvenir, he said, and he'd tried to preserve it with formaldehyde but the sergeant, who checked everyone's papers before letting them pass onto the ship bound for home, wouldn't let him take it, and there was a ruckus while they tried to decide how to dispose of the arm. Charles pondered the humor of all those men who had killed other soldiers with bayonets, had run through fiery fields where dead bodies and body parts lay all around them, all those men so disgusted by that arm and confused about what to do with it. Someone suggested that they throw it to the dogs, who were starving anyway: "It's an enemy arm after all, not like we have to bury it or anything." And Charles laughed then, thinking about how appalled everyone had been, even he had been, at the thought of tossing that arm out to the dogs. But of course the formaldehyde would have killed the dogs, so the arm had to be taken by someone in charge onto the ship and thrown overboard, no one caring if the formaldehyde killed a few fish. Charles wondered out loud how many dogs had eaten the carrion of the battlefields before the bodies could be buried. Duane just looked at him then and mentioned that the storm was getting heavy, and Charles had to leave his wagon in town and walk home through the storm.

He relished the adventure and felt strong and healthy as he walked into the wind, thinking of home. It was after dark when he finally saw the light burning in a window, hoping it was his own, but it was a neighbor's he was lucky to reach that night, and they put him up until he could have the daylight to find the road home. In the swirling storm he had walked around in circles and spent the night at the edge of the town he had left hours earlier. He could have been lost in the night and frozen to death, the folks told him, and he thanked them for being there and laughed, telling them he had been thinking about the war that afternoon and maybe remembering how he'd survived that helped him survive the storm. By then he could take his wagon, and he arrived home in time for breakfast. Rose and Mary had worried themselves to sleep and were making plans to come into the town to ask about him and they were glad he had spent the night safely. "I knew you'd make it okay because you always did," said Rose, and he hugged her and told her it was thinking about her wonderful letters that had saved him, that her letters were magic and she was an angel who made his life so worth living he couldn't die. Rose made herself a vow, which she meant for the moment, to be faithful to him.

Duane found someone to help his grandparents in the store and left to seek his fortune, literally, like the boys in the stories who go off on adventures to grow up, learn many secrets and find wealth so they can return to claim the imprisoned princess who waits and yearns. Counting on his strength and determination and, yes, his persuasive good looks, to get work wherever he went, he went everywhere: Chicago, Omaha, Denver, San Francisco and Seattle and all kinds of towns in between. He was gone for two years and kept in touch with his grandma in the belief that Rose would ask about him. He wanted her to write to him but didn't stay long enough or predictably enough to even ask, so he was spared the disappointment of not hearing from her.

He met some women along the way and enjoyed brief encounters, passing himself off as the wandering adventurer whom no woman could tie down, but of course that was his cover for being hopelessly in love with the one woman he couldn't have. He had fallen in love not only with Rose of Sharon but with the image of himself as part of a tragic triangle.

Sharon was relieved that he was gone and settled back into what was routine for herself and her family. She was good to Charles and Mary for a while, then fell into the kind of depression that drained the very life out of her and sat for days at a time not talking or walking, just breathing, maybe not even seeing the two of them as they came to her with offerings of food, tales, assistance. It got so bad that Rose of Sharon wouldn't even make the trip to the outhouse and soiled herself, and Charles had to clean her up and that was when he took her back to the hospital near Roanoke, broken hearted that she would miss the blooming of the garden, for he knew that Rose dearly loved her garden. Mary was old enough to care for it, knew what were weeds and what would grow and bloom into colorful flowers, and she took care of the garden with all the love and attention she would like to have enjoyed. It was her gift to her mother who returned when the garden had bloomed and begun to wither in the summer heat. The tulips were already gone and the daffodils, but the marigolds were coming in, the day lilies continued strong, and Mary fed and watered the roses so they would hold their heads up for the return of their mistress. That's what Mary called her mother when she came home, pale and weak, but at least smiling: The mistress of the roses. Everyday Mary went out and picked some of the flowers she had so carefully cultivated for a bouquet for her mother's room. Of course the flowers, once picked, did not last long in their vases, and so they would be thrown out and new blooms sacrificed to the daily ritual of cheering up her mother. As a special favor, she sometimes let her father take the bouquet inside. Rose of Sharon stayed indoors most of the summer and then finally went out in August and was so struck by the beauty of the place that she lamented out loud having missed so much time. But it was okay. They spent hours hiking in the woods and finding all the exquisite wild things that grew hidden in the bushes, in the mosses underfoot, along the sides of the creek. Mary would run around, while her mother found a comfortable seat on a rock or within the curve of large tree roots, and find things to show her and delight her and they wouldn't return to the house until the sun was so low in the sky that they began to feel the slightest tinge of cold and an exciting fear of the dark. Then they would run and arrive breathless and happy and even laughing, because they were safe.

And once again, Charles would believe that the sad times were over and this contentment would last forever. Mary knew better, but she also knew not to tell him: it would serve no purpose.

Charles had begun to sell furniture that he built and carved decoratively with flowers and vines. He had taken a few pieces to White Sulphur Springs, where wealthy folks came from all along the east coast to enjoy the springs at the hotel and resort there, and those pieces had sold well, and the shopkeeper who had taken them ordered more. Mary loved to watch her father carve the delicate designs in the grained and pliant oak. Sometimes he would ask her what flowers now? Roses? Lilies? Daisies? But Mary always asked for roses, and that was mostly what Charles carved. He named his line of furniture as the shopkeeper called it, the Rose Collection, and he signed each piece because the shopkeeper told him he could get more money if he signed them. It got so Charles spent more time carving furniture than farming and finally gave up trying to grow any cash crop. The furniture, mostly rocking chairs, became his cash crop. He would travel to White Sulphur with a wagonload of pieces every few weeks and when it was nice, he invited Rose and Mary to go with him. Mary had already been, so she was excited at the prospect of showing her mother the grand hotel and maybe have lunch there with some of the money the shopkeeper gave them. They would get all dressed up.

And so they did, and Rose looked far more beautiful than any of the wealthy women, young or old, who walked purposively through the lobbies and hallways of the hotel, to their rooms, to the lobby for tea, to meet friends, on their way to eat some sumptuous meal in one of the restaurants. Everyone looked at Rose admiringly. Her dress, that she had made herself, was simple but elegant and made of good fabric. And yet, Rose felt out of place in the gracious colonial hotel. She got flustered and hurried about, looking for the way out, and getting lost because the back and the front entrances were both equally elegant and she forgot which side they had come in on.

Mary and Charles had to hurry to catch up with her and take her hands on both sides and guide her back to the side from which they came, and they walked her around the grounds for a while, trying to calm her down and talk her into trying the buffet. "I thought you would like it," said Charles. "I thought this was just the kind of place you always dream of being." And of course that was just it. Rose did always dream of being in just such a place, not for an hour or a day but always, for her lifetime, and it hurt her too badly to be there, where she knew she belonged, and have to leave. But as she tried to explain to Charles in a way that wouldn't hurt his feelings, she saw that nothing would not hurt his feelings unless she went inside and ate a hearty luncheon and complimented him on the treat, so she did that time pull herself together and do that very thing, even though she felt sicker and sicker with each bite, and when gentlemen came by to tell Charles that he was a lucky man to have two such lovely ladies with him, and Charles would smile and greet them and thank them, Rose looked down at her plate and stifled her anger. Her father had always said it was harder for a rich man to get into heaven than for a camel to pass through the eye of a needle, but Rose of Sharon knew he didn't really mean it, he was just bitter that the luck of the draw had not been good to his own, and she had to admit the distribution of wealth was an unfair puzzlement. As a child she had dreamed of a prince carrying her off like Cinderella to some castle (just exactly like this White Sulphur Springs Resort) and then she had to learn that such dreams were unattainable and scale her dreams down to what was at least within the realm of her reality. This place just brought up too much childhood pain.

They sold quilts at the shop where Charles took his rockers and vanities, and Rose got the idea of making quilts for the shop to sell. She began to join the sewing bee group again, much to their surprise, and she was modest and gracious with them, and even Duane's grandma forgave her for using them in the past. And Rose also began to go to church, apologetically at first, since she had not gone before. Rose sincerely wanted to become a better wife to Charles, for she had seen his heartbreak when he couldn't please her and his joy when she pretended that he had, and it hurt to think she had never really loved or appreciated him enough. He didn't care that much for church himself, but it pleased him when they went as a family and it was easier for Rose to please him in this way than by trying to talk to him about her feelings, which she herself didn't quite understand. Rose thought perhaps she might be settling down inside and she was glad, for she'd never meant to hurt anyone.

Then Duane came home. Charles saw him at the store and mentioned it to Rose, who was kneading dough for bread and didn't look up. She knew her face got red and hot when he said the man's name, and she hoped he didn't see. She was careful then not to go into town with Charles, saying she preferred to stay and work in the garden. But then Duane came to church and tried to catch her eye. She refused to look at him, so he approached the entire family and talked to Charles a while, trying to figure out why Rose made no secretive effort to talk to him privately. He showed off for her, telling Charles about all the cities he'd been to and that he intended to go back to Seattle to live, and found a nice house and now all he needed was a wife. He talked so long that it was Rose who had to tell Charles that they should be getting home. Finally in desperation, Duane went to the farm to find Sharon alone when he knew Charles was making a delivery to White Sulphur Springs. She didn't want Mary to see him with her and told him he must leave, but he made her promise to meet him in the shed that night after Mary went to bed, after Charles was asleep. He would wait. So Rose of Sharon made dinner for her family, knowing that her old lover was hiding in the shed, and she read Mary a bedtime story and even made love with Charles and then when her husband and her daughter were asleep, she got up quietly and dressed and went out to tell the young man that she never wanted to see him again.

Charles heard a noise outside. No matter how softly she walked, Rose couldn't help the porch creaking. Charles thought a prowler threatened his family and got up, put his pants on and grabbed his shotgun. He left the house and looked around and thought he may have heard someone in the shed.

Duane reached out to Sharon and was reaching still when Charles shot him. His blood spattered Sharon's face and chest, and Mary, running to the shed and seeing the blood on her mother's dress, thought it was her mother who was shot, and Rose of Sharon, feeling herself bleeding inside, feeling her life ebb away into a chaos that couldn't be heaven and must be hell, thought that Charles should have shot her, and Charles, seeing the grief on her face, did, aiming straight for the heart.

Rose of Sharon sank to her knees and tried to say the words "I'm sorry," but the shots were still ringing in Mary's ears, and all she saw were her mother's hands reaching heavenward.

"A crime of passion," they called it, and Charles was a war hero and born in their county, never mind he'd disappeared all those years and his mother was Indian. Charles was one of them and did what anyone of them would have done, finding a wife with a lover. So Charles was free to go, to mourn, to raise his daughter and try to get through his life.

X

When it was all over, Mary lay still in her own blood and looked at the snowy landscape outside her window. It was a late spring snow and covered the tulips and daffodils that had already bloomed in the yard. It was a soft white blanket that covered the ground and the flowers and the budding trees and its whiteness blended with the whiteness of the sky. As she looked at the tangle of branches that leaned toward each other, weighted down with the snow, she let her eyes follow the delicate tracery of black lines, the dark wet undersides of the branches, that seemed etched on the sky as exquisitely as the lines of silver frost on the windows in the deepest cold of winter.

But it warmed up on this spring day and the sun emerged, pale at first and then brighter and finally began to melt the snow and the colors of the flowers came through at last. The red tulips looked like drops of blood on the white blanket of snow. Mary herself felt as if a soft and numbing blanket had been laid over her and she could not move her legs or arms, only her eyes, and she drifted off to sleep, dreamless, and when she awoke it was completely dark in her room and outside her window.

At first she experienced the familiar regret of having missed the daylight that she always felt when she fell asleep in the afternoon, and then she remembered that this day something unspeakable had happened to her, and it was her poor unhappy father who had done it. But Mary remembered, with some effort, wondering if it was memory or imagination, that he had done something terrible to her mother as well. Sometimes she forgot, thinking that her mother was simply away for a while as she had been often enough. It was frightening to Mary that her memories, even of that very morning, could be so deeply buried so quickly, and that she could be so confused about her own life. It had been a relief when her father refused to send her to school, because she was afraid of talking to the other children about herself. She never knew how to answer questions whether from the children or the teachers, and they all thought there was something wrong with her mind. Sometimes she was afraid they were right, even though she could read better than most. But then sometimes she got confused and felt like she lived in the stories she read, the stories were more real to her than her own life that she contemplated, when at all, as if through a fathom of water.

She was only twelve that day but felt as tired and bone weary as a

Sanchez

grandmother. She first curled up on her side and tried to go back to sleep, but then her father called her to fix dinner, and she had to get up slowly and walk painfully and with difficulty to the basin and begin to clean herself.

Her father said nothing while she prepared the evening meal and nothing while he ate, but when he finished, he complimented her on her cooking and said to her softly, as if remembering her name for the first time, "Mary Queen of Scots. What a beautiful name. And you are as lovely as your name, as lovely as the flowers in the garden, the loveliest flower of all. You know that I love you?" And Mary could say only a quiet "yes" and then she watched him for a clue to what would happen next.

Nothing happened, and Mary was not sure how to end the day, so she asked her father if he remembered the last Christmas, what they had done and he remembered it fondly and reminded her about it, and feeling encouraged, Mary asked him about the Christmas before that and again he remembered it fondly and reminded her of what they had done and the gifts he had made for her. So then Mary asked him about the Christmas before that, and her father became angry, wondering why she kept asking about Christmases and remembering that the last one she asked about was only a few months after Rose of Sharon had died, had died, had died. He didn't want to remember how and why he had killed her. He told Mary to stop chattering, to stop bothering him, and he went out into the night to walk in the woods.

So Mary kept track of the years since her father shot her mother by remembering the subsequent Christmases. Sometimes she would whisper the litany to herself, reciting the gifts, whether there had been snow or not, whether they had gone to a neighbor's house to eat and what had been served. In this way she kept her life in order and would do so until she died in 1960, each year adding the new details and rehearsing them so she would never forget. Whatever else she might forget, she kept track of the memories of those days when the mundane horrors of everyday life were set aside and everyone worked at joy.

When her mother was alive the garden had been a family effort under her mother's supervision, but now her father never went into the garden. He spent almost all daylight hours in his workshop, where he made the furniture that he sold in White Sulphur and only came to the house to eat his meals and never went outside at all during the days. Mary heard him get up in the night to wander the woods in the dark, and sometimes she watched out her window to see him disappear up the road in the moonlight and said a little child's prayer for his safe return. After the terrible thing happened, she continued to look after him and pray for him with the same love and pity she had always felt for her lovesick father. She thought perhaps in his pain and confusion that he sometimes thought she was her mother. Certainly in the dark of night, in the haze of too much whiskey or simply too much pain, this was possible. So reasoned Mary, longing to love her father and trying to understand the terrible thing that had been done.

Sometimes she wondered if she had done something to bring it on herself. She had begun to develop breasts and bleed once a month. She knew she was a woman now, but she knew that she didn't feel like a woman. She had felt old since she was a young child, but she was not comfortable with the idea of being a woman. She wanted to be that wise old child forever, and she hated it when the boys in town looked at her and tried to flirt with her and laughed at her when she would not flirt back. Now when she went to town with her father, she stuck close to his side and kept her eyes on the ground, and if the boys wanted to try to flirt with her, let them face her father. When she went into town with her father, she felt protected and began to think that maybe what he had done to her was not so terrible, because he truly did love her and now he would make sure that no one else ever touched her that way. Mary read the Bible through and through with a great attention to detail, and she knew that in the Bible, fathers lay with daughters. She wanted to ask the preacher about it, ask him about Noah for instance, and then she could find out what he thought without giving anything away. For her father hadn't said much, but one thing he had said, and that was that she was never to tell anyone about what had happened. "They will take you away from me," he had said and didn't tell her who the "they" was. Anymore it seemed that the whole world was "they."

By the time Mary went to church again with her father the terrible thing had happened again, and she was so worried that the preacher would see into her mind that she didn't have the nerve to ask him about Noah. The second time had been at night in the dark, and Mary had pretended to be asleep and then she did fall asleep and tried to imagine that it had been a dream, but her father's silence at the breakfast table told her it had happened. He almost seemed about to apologize, but couldn't, and brought her some wildflowers at dinner. By then the wild laurel blossoms were all over the woods like exotic miniature orchids. Mary knew all about orchids and read about them and knew that her mother had dreamed about having a roomful of them. Mary loved to see these orchid-like flowers in the woods and wished her father wouldn't be picking them, because they wilted within hours, even in water, but of course she thanked him over and over and made a fuss over his gift because she couldn't stand to see his pain. He was so sorry, so sad.

The next day, Mary began to prepare the garden for planting. She had a map in her head of where everything would go and measured off her design with footsteps in circles. The sweet peas going in first along with the onions went around the outer edges, and she would arrange everything else in concentric circles until the middle where she would plant the tomatoes ringed with marigolds. In between each row of vegetables, Mary planned flowers. Like her mother, Mary could not get enough of flowers. Her father came in for the evening meal and stood a while watching her pacing off the circles and he seemed puzzled, but didn't say anything. "We'll be having fresh greens soon," she told her father as if nothing unusual had happened.

After that second time, her father always came to her in the dark of night and after a while Mary became accustomed to his visits. She would pretend she was sleeping and dreaming, and neither of them talked about it. When she finally felt up to asking the preacher about Noah, he simply expressed his astonishment and disapproval of a girl so young reading that particular part of the Bible and recommended other readings to her. So Mary knew it was absolutely wrong and that she was all alone in the world with no one she could talk to about anything. But by then, Mary had reasoned that most of what occurred among human beings in the world was wrong. It was only in heaven that there existed any hope of right living and true happiness and that was the point after all, wasn't it? All this singing and praying on Sundays? She would watch all the people in church and be able to tell by their expressions from one week to the next who was in trouble or harboring evil secrets. No one was pure, no one without shame, no one truly happy, even though everyone pretended to be all those things. It was a lesson that seeped into her soul and made her kind, judging no one harshly, not even herself.

The pea vines were flowering and the radish leaves were coming up by the time it was warm enough to plant the squash and pumpkin seeds. Mary spent days squatting on the warm crumbly earth, building mounds and arranging the seeds carefully around them. She imagined the large leafed vines dancing around the garden like the designs that framed the mirrors of the oak dressers her father built and carved, and she planned how she would plant the corn stalks and then arrange the tomatoes around them so the tomato vines could climb the corn stalks. Mary thought that was a very inventive way to support the tomato plants. She looked forward to dinners of juicy tomatoes with tender new potatoes and sweet young corn. She worked without noticing the time until the sun was low in the sky and she was suddenly chilled and then, as she rose, she saw her father watching her.

By the time it was warm enough to set out the tomato plants, the rest of the garden was growing in a noticeable pattern of concentric circles, and her father, who had been watching her planting as if he was watching some intricate dance step, asked her why she had planted the garden that way. "I just wanted to make a design with it the way you make designs when you carve in wood." He wondered if anyone had told her about the idea or if she had dreamed it perhaps one night. "No, it just occurred to me when I went out to the garden. Do you like it?" And Charles seemed confused, not expecting to be asked if he liked it. "It's very pretty," he said and then looked down at his plate, ate quickly and went up to bed and to sleep before Mary had even finished washing up the dishes. Usually he sat up by the lamp and read some, sometimes out loud. But this night he fell to sleep almost before it was completely dark, and later Mary heard him crying and choking on his tears. She got up and went to his bed and asked him if he was alright, and he said he would be alright and told her to go back to bed, and she reached out to touch his head, but that made him cry harder, that unexpected touch of gentle sympathy, and he controlled his sobbing enough to tell her again to go back to bed, and so she did. Mary lay awake all that night, listening to the choking sounds until she also had to cry, but quietly, so he wouldn't know she was listening. She heard him groan and whisper her mother's name, and she heard him whisper another name she didn't recognize, and she recognized her own name when once he whispered that too, the whole long name: Mary Queen of Scots. Such an odd name, her teachers had said, such a funny name, the boys in town had laughed. But Mary loved her name.

Mary slept late the next morning and when she awoke, her father sat on her bedside and was watching her face. When she opened her eyes, he stroked her hair and smiled and said he was taking the day off to go fishing and invited her to go along with him. He seemed well rested and well he might, having cried himself into a deep sleep that lasted well into the mid-morning. It was a rainy day, a good day for fishing, and a good day for hiking in the woods, which were fragrant with the fresh smells of pine and sassafras brought up by the rain. They put on high boots and layers of warm clothes and walked into the cathedral-like opening beneath tall oaks that bent towards each other high above them, filtering the sunlight and the rain alike, creating a sheltered world in which grew delicate ferns, soft mosses, every kind of mushroom, lacy lichens and tiny wildflowers that a man had to kneel to see. They left the road and disappeared into the forest, climbing hills and down again until they found the spring that flowed forth from a cave and followed that flow to the wide pools that formed sometimes this side of an old willow, sometimes the other side, from one season to another, and there they fished for trout, small and tender, that they would steam and eat, head and all, that night for supper. It was a joyful day for them, for Mary had learned to take her pleasure when she could, and Charles was trying to follow her example.

The next day everything in the garden was a good head taller Charles said, and Mary laughed and set about to weed, for the weeds grew twice as fast as the flowers and vegetables, as everyone in the county would be glad to tell you.

Surrounded by such fecundity, it was inevitable that Mary, too, should bear, and no sooner had she finished the planting that she noticed that the monthly bleeding had stopped almost as soon as it had started, for it had only just started. Mary would not even have known what it meant but for having cared for her mother during those times of month. Had she not been nursing her mother, her mother might not have told her anything about it. That was how Mary learned everything in life; by accident.

She didn't want to tell her father right away, and she knew he would be upset because how then could they keep the secret? It never occurred to her to let folks think it was a boy her own age, and it certainly never occurred to her that her father might think that it was. For the summer she decided not to tell him, not to think about it even, for it was not something she had any control over. She spent her mornings working in her garden and the afternoons as they got hotter and hotter, walking in the cool forest. She liked to find the creeks and sit on a rock feeling the draft that came up from the rushing water. The energy from the creek made her feel clean and she would breath it in to clean her insides too.

Her father never asked her about where she went every afternoon, until the fall when her belly grew in contrast with her small, thin limbs, and she could no longer hide the fact that she was pregnant. Then he became very angry and asked her about boys in town, boys whose names she didn't even recognize, but he didn't believe that and insisted on knowing who the father was, as if nothing had ever happened between them. Mary found it hard to say, but she finally said, very quietly, crying through her words, that the child was his, of course, whose else could it be? Would it be? But his, his, his.

The secret was out, because they had treated it like a secret, had never talked about it, this thing that happened in the dark of night while Charles was drunk and Mary pretended to be sleeping. He had pretended something too, Mary didn't know what, perhaps that it never really happened and now he was confronted with the proof that yes, without any doubt, this thing had happened, because Charles knew that Mary didn't really know those boys in town, had kept her eyes on the ground and let him protect her from them.

Charles stopped his furious questions suddenly in the middle of a breath and caught his breath and turned away from Mary and into the woods, into the dark places where animals lived and magic existed and his mother's spirit still wandered, he was certain. He did not come back until morning, and Mary prayed for him, for his safe return, for she loved him still, strongly and fearfully, promising to take the blame, casting about in her mind for a way to keep the terrible secret. She could not go to church anymore for her condition betrayed not just her father but everyone there, threatened to expose the abyss of evil that everyone hid so carefully behind the smiles of contentment and righteous talk…everyone had something to hide and bringing one secret out in the open would threaten all of them. Mary knew this and thought long and hard, trying to think of a way to hide, a story to tell, something the town could accept. But she couldn't discuss this with her father, for they had never discussed this terrible thing, had never acknowledged it and she knew he needed to pretend it had never happened, just as she had pretended to be sleeping when it did. She would ask her father to take her away to another place, maybe the place where she had been born, far away from here. Even in the frenzy and fear of her thoughts, she already regretted the garden, the waste of it. When Charles returned at dawn, he found her sleeping among the pumpkins, covered with vines, crawling with ladybugs.

Charles had gone to the cave and asked for a dream to guide him now that his daughter was pregnant with his child. He had slept there in the mouth of the cave and dreamed of carefully cutting her throat and then he dreamed that he was drowning. In his dream, he fought first for breath and then let his body be carried by the flow of the river, until he was surrounded by gray water and gray skies and rain, and he heard his mother's voice and thought he must have already died, but he woke up with the sun in his eyes and went to find Mary. He knew that to save her from the boys in the town, he would have to carefully cut her throat and let the river carry her away and he would let the river take him too, and they would both be free and both be safe, for this was a cruel world, a sad world, and he couldn't protect her anymore.

Charles never loved his child more than when he gently lifted her from the garden and carried her to the river. She slept in his arms, exhausted with thinking, with fearing, with planning and praying. He had picked the last roses from the garden and put these into her hands, she grasped them in her sleep, oblivious to the thorns that pierced her skin and tiny veins and oblivious to the blood that streamed down her hands and arms as her father carried her to the river that would be her grave. He held her close to him as he walked in long strides, stepping over rocks and small ravines and snakes that wound, sluggish with cold, toward their winter holes. The day grew colder with each step he took, and then they were there at the river and he lovingly lay her on the ground in a thicket of wild mint, and he took out a knife that he had sharpened so he would not cause her pain, and he carefully cut her throat, feeling a magical strength and sureness in his cold benumbed hands. Carefully, he held her lovely head and carefully, he made the cut. Then he walked with her into the middle of the river and set her adrift upon the current. Then he aimed his knife at his own innards and fell into it and into the river, which carried him down, and down, and down, under the roots of trees and around boulders, and he was never seen again.

But Mary's light body drifted toward the banks of the river, gently on the surface of the water, and in the morning sun she shone luminous, and in the morning sun she appeared as a miraculous vision to the young John Banks, who had been camping by the river and just that very morning had been praying for a miracle.

XI

When Charles thought he was sending his daughter to the safety of the next world, he was halfway there himself and his cold hand missed its mark. She bled slightly from the wound on the neck, but the cold water soon stopped the blood. The river itself, which had taken her grandmother, rejected her young spirit and carried her to the safety of John Banks's arms, for he was waiting for a miracle that morning. Seeing her pale body floating obediently downriver, he assumed she had passed on and was overjoyed when he pulled her out and she came to, slowly, sluggishly, but very much alive. He sang a lot of loud praises to the Lord that morning, while the confused and terrified child watched him, wondering in the back of her mind where her father was and if he was coming to get her. John Banks had not seen her father's body, which had been washed down a different fork of the river and disappeared, so he couldn't answer her questions and he was in no mood to ponder earthly questions anyway and thought she was asking about the great father, the one holy father, who art in heaven, so what John Banks had to say to Mary made no sense to her. She was so cold and glad to have him wrap her in a blanket and when he helped her up into his wagon, she thought he might take her home where she would wait for her father, and she told him as best she could where she was from, although it was hard, because she didn't know where she was. But none of that mattered to John Banks, for by the time he helped her into his wagon, he had noticed that she was with child and when he asked her about the father of her child, she had said only that she had not been with anyone. Then it all became clear as day to John Banks, who had been praying for a miracle for years now, trying to work his power on domestic animals, curing the livestock of local farmers and getting paid for it when, by accident, a calf or a goat recovered from its illness and took off beneath his ordinary hands. He preached too and gathered a few desperate followers, who supported him with their gifts of cash, or food, or a place to sleep for the night as he traveled around and around the country, always coming back to the county of his birth, his miraculous birth, to hear his family tell it.

But his birth was the last miracle his family was willing to believe in, and he knew they would never believe this one, no, two: the death and resurrection and the virgin birth. He had with him the pure child chosen by God to deliver unto the people the son of God, a second time as, of course, the Bible predicted

Sanchez

time and time again. That night by the firelight he looked through his worn little Bible and read passage after passage to Mary, whose very name portended the great event, but she didn't think much of it, didn't see it at first and kept asking about her father and when he would return her to him. "Your father isn't ready to receive you just yet, little girl. You have great and important work to do here on earth first," an answer that thoroughly puzzled Mary. She began to panic then and wanted him to leave her to find her own way home, and John reassured her then that he was taking her to her father but first she had to give birth to the child she carried, and then she could return to her father whenever she wanted to and she realized that he was right, for her father had gotten angry at her when he realized she carried a child within her, and she agreed it was best to wait and was grateful to John Banks, who offered to take care of her during her pregnancy.

The first thing they did was travel to a town far from where John Banks's family would be likely to find them, and he began to tell the story of finding the girl in the river and bringing her back to life and how she carried God's own child within her, and some folks thought he was crazy, but others were convinced, because John Banks could talk himself into a veritable fever and be very convincing to those folks inclined to believe in such things. "He's the real thing," they would say, not fully understanding what kind of reality they were talking about. And folks were poor then, dirt poor, hopelessly poor, and a miracle of some kind was what each and every one of his followers needed badly, some kind of miracle, any kind of miracle. So John Banks came to them at exactly the right time with just exactly the right promise. They, one or two, then ten and twenty, rallied around him, waiting for this miracle, because by the time John Banks reached them, they had nothing to lose and might just as well believe in his promise as someone else's. They'd believed the promises of politicians and look where that had gotten them, and they had believed the promises of their hearts when they had needed to hope that they could somehow make a life out of the land, the bedrock, the barren, rocky land, the beautiful, fickle land that they had acquired so easily but kept at their peril, afraid to venture forth to greener pastures, until there were no greener pastures to venture forth to, and look where that had gotten them, so why not believe the promise of this preacher with his young innocent virgin, why not? And some went further than that and believed it with fervor, with joyous piety, because it was true, it was true and it was a sin not to believe in the truth, hadn't they always been told?

So John Banks and Mary Queen of Scots traveled around the countryside together, and little by little it dawned on Mary what this John Banks fellow was up to, and at first it frightened her but then it intrigued her, and she did

100

like all the attention and awe. People gave them money, for what, she couldn't rightly tell, and John Banks bought her beautiful ready-made dresses, dresses with high necks trimmed in lace and long sleeves with lace trim and empire waists that left room for the baby growing inside her, but still gave her figure an elegant line. He brought her flowers to put in her long blonde hair, fine, baby fine hair she had, and he admired her hair, her skin, her eyes, but he never laid a hand on her, never suggested anything indecent, for he truly believed that Mary carried the son of God in her womb, and he perceived her, plain girl that she was, a great beauty because she was blessed with grace and that was the true beauty of woman, to be beloved of God. He would talk like that for hours and get carried away with the music of his words, and Mary would get carried away too, listening as it if to music, not making any particular sense of what he said, but soothed to hear him say it. He told her once it wasn't sense that people looked for in a preacher but rhythm, and that was why words sung had more impact than words spoken, but when he, John Banks, spoke the words of his heart, it was like singing, and surely Mary had to agree with that. And Mary did agree with that and she would sway, enraptured, when John Banks preached to his followers, and the followers who would clap and chant amen would see her in that state of otherworldly grace, and they knew that she, Mary Queen of Scots, was the real thing, too. They didn't call her that of course, no sense in offending the Irish, the English, the Italians, the Germans among the followers. John Banks was impressed with the name her mother had chosen to give her, but advised her that from now on it was best she be called simply Mary, the universal Mary, the Mary that all the followers could adopt as their own.

And they did. All through the cold winter, Mary and John Banks were the guests of farmers and miners who fed them their best and stoked up the fires, using more wood than they should have to show hospitality to the holy travelers. All had their stories of hard times and Mary listened with sympathy, but helpless, and John Banks didn't really listen, waiting for their stories to end so he could preach to them, stoke the emotional fires that would keep him warm in their hearts and make them generous. John Banks preached from habit, not always feeling God in him, but pretending he felt God in him, so he would be ready when the time came; so in that way John Banks really did have faith. And he really honestly believed that Mary was his miracle. Sometimes she said things that made him think this was just another young girl in trouble, but he stifled his misgivings and forged on spreading the good news, because the people needed good news, not least of all himself; he needed good news as much as anyone. And the home brew helped keep the fires stoked too. John and his followers always drank a lot of the home brewed wine and brandy that made them feel festive. He let it be known as well that he didn't believe God frowned on moonshiners as much as some would have them think, because… and then he would pull out his Bible and quote all the places he had marked that spoke of the fruit of the vine, taking the fruit of the vine to cover moonshine as well as the wine fermenting behind the wood stoves of his followers' sitting rooms.

Mary never stopped praying for her father and missing him, but she came to see John Banks as a father too, although he was younger than her father and seemed to be on the verge of drunk almost all of the time. She half expected him to come to her in the night, but he never did and she began to sleep easier after the first couple of months. She even said something to him on a couple of occasions that should have clued him in, but by then he was too euphoric, or drunk, or both to put two and two together about her father and her son.

Around Christmas time John Banks talked about going to visit his Auntie Ada and debated whether or not to take Mary with him. He knew without even thinking about it that his Auntie Ada would assume the girl was his lover and the baby was his, and nothing he could say from his heart or the Bible would change her mind. So John Banks found a place to leave Mary for Christmas while he went back home to spend a couple days with his aunt, who had raised him and his father. The folks who put Mary up were kind and tried to include her in the family celebration, confused as to how exactly she should figure into it, being she was the mother of the second Christ, or would be giving birth to the second coming, or however it went, they really needed John Banks to explain it to them, how this was supposed to be happening. Mary was more confused than they were and forlorn and lonely, spending her first Christmas away from home. But she comforted herself with the thought that in a few months she would have her own child, who she would take everywhere with her, wherever she had to travel, and would never be lonely again. At 13, she looked forward to a companion as much or more than to a son. No one ever discussed the possibility that the child could be a girl. Later, when she was tallying Christmases, she would tell her son that that Christmas was their first Christmas together.

When John Banks came back to get her, he asked her when she expected the baby to be born, and Mary really didn't have a clue, but the woman who was taking them in for a while speculated by the looks of her, that it would be a spring baby, coming out just about the same time as the calves and other farm animals, and they all agreed that was a good sign, very appropriate. Mary remembered back to her garden, how she had planted each thing in its turn and in circles of color and scent, and she missed having a garden and picking her supper fresh. Her hostess was only too glad to invite her to return then and partake of her garden, welcome to help plant it if she liked. But Mary said she'd be going home to her father then, and the woman looked at John Banks puzzled and sad, thinking Mary meant her father in heaven, and John Banks gestured that silence was the best response at that moment. Then her husband broke in and asked where the birthing would take place, and John Banks answered that the spot would be revealed in due time, and the plain farming man offered to let them build something up on the hill behind his house. That field got a lot of sun and it was high up and the followers could camp below and wait for the glorious event. And John Banks responded that God had spoken through his servant Elmer Baker, and the next day they visited a neighbor who had a sawmill and talked him into giving them some lumber, and while John Banks traveled through several counties to spread the word of where and when the great event was going to happen, the farmer and his neighbors built a barnlike structure with a chimney, where Mary could spend the rest of her pregnancy sitting by her own woodstove. Although it was high on the hill, there was a spring higher still and they piped the clear spring water down to a cistern by he cabin, as they had taken to calling it, and folks brought pitchers and tubs and quilts and a hand-hewn bed with a feather mattress, and every day someone came up the hill with food for Mary and then, when he came back, for John, who still slept in his wagon, away from Mary so everyone could see that he didn't touch her that way. And so she lived like that, in a kind of shrine for the rest of the winter, until by late February, she was so big she could hardly walk, and then in March as the first spring flowers started to poke out from the snow, Mary went into labor.

People had been gathering, making campsites all over the hill since the end of February, building fires to keep warm and making gifts for a child. One man carved puppets out of wood, a woman brought cans of pickles, another a cloth bag of dried flowers and spices. There were embroidered pillows and hand crocheted, lace-trimmed linens, knitted baby blankets, mittens and booties, just like a baby shower, Mary thought. Everyone wanted to be a part of this, and it was strange, because Mary remembered that at home everyone always wanted to be part of any birth, any ordinary birth, for no birth was deemed ordinary. Everyone at home made gifts for the new babies and celebrated when the baby was born healthy and the mother lived, and mourned if one or the other or both died in the process. Birth was a miracle. Mary asked John Banks, wasn't birth always a miracle anyway? And he pondered her question for a while and then just said that this was different, but Mary couldn't really see that it was.

People came with guitars and banjos and fiddles and every night there was music by the campfires. And some reporters came from newspapers around the state, and John Banks would talk to them but wouldn't let them talk to Mary. Mary was just as glad not to talk to them, for she was getting worried her father would find out about what was going on and come and take her home and be angry that she was passing herself off as someone special, but then again, she knew he wouldn't want her telling anyone that the child she carried was her father's child, her earthly father's child. So Mary kept quiet and let John Banks do all the lying, or was it lying? Certainly he knew more than she did. Sometimes she pretended it wasn't happening, and sometimes she pretended she believed John Banks, and sometimes she pretended she didn't know what to believe, but underneath it all, she wanted to go home and cried quietly in the cold pre-dawn hours, when the campfires glowed low to the ground and the music was but a faint reverberation in her head.

Then one night she heard a voice, a loud clear voice, a man's voice it sounded like, and the voice said, "Your father is dead," and that was that. Mary knew it was true even though she didn't know where the voice had come from. Now she knew she would never go home again and she would have to travel forever with John Banks all around the land lying to people and the thought scared her, but she couldn't think of anywhere else she could go. She told John Banks about the voice, and his heart went cold.

But John Banks put his best face on things, and walked out among the followers camped all over the hillside, more of them with each passing day, some believers, some gawkers, some attracted to a good time wherever a good time was to be had, and he preached to the followers, preparing them for the great event despite some dread he felt in his heart.

When Mary's labor began there were many midwives among the followers to assist her in the birth, and she needed help to be sure, for it was a long and painful labor beginning at dawn one day and not ending until dawn the next. The midwives took turns watching, encouraging and helping her and there were moments when they thought they might lose her or the baby, or both, and John Banks was already thinking about what he would say if such an event were to occur. But the baby was born alive to a weak but healthy young mother. Problem was, the baby had no arms.

The first midwife to know this was the one who had reached up inside Mary to feel if the baby's head was in the right position. It didn't feel right, the baby's body, but the woman thought it couldn't be what she thought and guided the baby out of the womb while the other women watched, holding their breath and letting it out all at once in unison. Then the baby was out and crying and fine in every way except that he didn't have arms. The women all looked at each other to confirm what each had seen and couldn't quite believe. Mary still didn't know. A second woman washed the baby and laid him on his mother's breast, quietly, not knowing what this could mean. The crowd was yelling, wanting to know if the baby was born, wanting to see the baby, yelling for the midwives to hold the baby up for them to see. Some started running up the hill to get a closer look, others held back in awe now that the baby was certainly born, it had to be, yes? No? When? What was happening? Even John Banks had kept his distance during the birth. But now he ran up the hill ahead of the followers to see this child, whose coming he had preached about now for so many months.

When John Banks saw the baby, he was speechless for the first time in his entire life, and just when words were most needed, words to explain this terrible turn of events, to turn the terrible into the awesome, the meaningful, the symbolic of something righteous. John Banks couldn't speak and let the crowd take over, rumoring that the child had no arms, and this could not possibly be the son of God; this had to be the child of the devil. Mary had passed out in exhaustion when the baby finally came out and lay peacefully with him on her breast, hearing the crowd as though from a great distance. And then they were all around her, crying and yelling and cursing John Banks who had lied to them, had taken them in, had led them into devil worship, for this was so clearly the work of Satan, and the crowd might have stoned them, John Banks and Mary and the baby and the midwives, but a few among them managed to turn them away, down the hill, back to their homes.

While the anger died down as the crowd dispersed, the midwives tried to comfort Mary, and Mary apologized to John Banks, who was too stunned to say much. One of the midwives talked about other such births she had witnessed and the others joined in to tell of their experiences, but neither Mary nor John Banks paid them much heed. The midwives stoked the fire and prepared some food and left them alone to ponder their future, now their followers had abandoned them. The man whose land they were living on came up the hill to tell them he didn't believe in all that devil stuff, but that he didn't feel safe in his community letting them stay there either. He was sorry for the girl, suspicious of the preacher. When he left, John Banks said his first words of the day. "The Lord will find a place for you," he said, and it scared Mary that he said "you" instead of "us." She felt herself about to be abandoned again and she didn't know where she could go with her baby, the beautiful, sweet, but strange, baby with no arms.

Mary named her son James because her father told her that he would have wanted to name her Jamie if she'd been born a boy, always hastening to add that he was glad she was a girl. The next day, John Banks went to talk to the farmer and ask if they could stay on the hill just a couple more days to give Mary time to recover from the long and difficult birth, and the farmer and his wife said of course, they wouldn't drive the child away and hinted that they hoped and expected she would be recovered soon. So John Banks left her up on the hill with the baby and one of the midwives came back to help her, bringing food with her, and John Banks was gone three days and three nights, which made Mary afraid he had already abandoned her.

But John Banks came back in a cheerful mood and told Mary, ah Mary Queen of Scots, such a wonderful name after all, that he had found a place for her and her baby James, but first he would baptize the baby, it was the least he could do.

So they went to the river, the river that had taken Mary's grandmother, had she but known it, and her father also, and given her to John Banks to save, for what, she wondered, and there they baptized the baby James.

Then John Banks drove Mary and James to another town over another mountain, where a traveling carnival had set up. They went into a tent and watched a man and several beautiful young women perform tricks on a high wire, and Mary Queen of Scots was thrilled to see this, never having seen anything like it in her life, but she wondered why in the midst of their troubles, John Banks would want to go to the circus. He didn't speak to her or look at her, so she sat quietly, enjoying the show with half her mind and half her heart and worrying about her future with the other half.

When the show inside the tent was over, Mary had seen many things for the first time, including a striped tiger and an elephant, which balanced balls on its trunk and then lifted the beautiful girls up high above the audience to deposit them on their aerial platform. Then they walked around and looked at the sideshows, a man who was twice as tall as any normal man, a fat woman with a very real looking beard and a two-headed calf. Then Mary understood that John Banks had found a place for her and her baby with no arms.

XII

No one at the carnival ever cried. They played strings instead: violins, a cello, guitars, dulcimers, lutes, banjos. They had an orchestra, and everyone played something. If you joined the Carnival della Strega and couldn't play a stringed instrument, you soon learned. The orchestra was the social life in the carnival, the freedom, the adventure, the joy, the hope and the despair as well. English and Italian were spoken there with many accents, but all the people spoke the dialect of some stringed music in unison at least once a week. Tatum, who had bought the carnival from the Italian family who still performed on the high wire, rarely gave permission for folks to leave on Sunday mornings to attend church in the towns they passed through, but he insisted on the Sunday afternoon orchestra practice and conducted with great passion, even though he himself could not read music. Hardly anyone could, all of them playing for the most part by ear and teaching each other the melodies of the folk music of their countries, or made something up. Sometimes a group of players who had been together a very long time could simply improvise together and come up with magnificent music, but never the same thing twice.

Those Sundays when they had performances they still got to practice, because Tatum had the wonderful idea that members of the troupe who were not actually costuming up or putting up the tents and cages should perform in small groups for the customers, who stood in line to buy their tickets and then stood in another line waiting to go in and find seats. There were the sideshows, of course, and James himself was one of them, but Tatum thought it added a touch of class to offer musical entertainment as well. When James was still an infant, Tatum allowed Mary to stay with him, watching over him and trying not to look at the gawkers who would have asked her all kinds of questions if they could but catch her eye. But as James grew older, she was required to leave him alone in his playpen set up on a platform and surrounded by mirrors behind high fence, and she played guitar on a little stage with three other women who played dulcimer, fiddle and banjo. They played some country music together, and then each played a solo that she made up on the spot, or a bit of some fancy classical piece that they had learned in the orchestra. The Bavarian aerialist had taught them all bits and pieces of Bach, Mozart, Brahms and Strauss. Later Mary would learn to play the cello, because James told her that he wished he had arms just so he could play the cello, he loved the

Stillbird

music of that instrument so much. So Mary, with little talent for it, struggled to learn the art of the cello, and James pretended to love the music she played so badly, because he knew she had done it for love of him; and what a strong and desperate love it was.

James couldn't play the cello with his legs but he did learn to do many other things with his feet and toes, such as writing and playing a special keyboard that Tatum had bought for him, and as he grew tall, with strong and graceful legs, he spent his days learning these tricks with which to entertain the crowds who came to see the freaks. He did not resent them and as he grew older and wise beyond his years, he talked while he performed his tricks and he had a great humor and a great compassion, and after a while it became apparent that the tricks were no longer necessary, because James could make people laugh or cry with his stories; stories that he made up simply by watching the people who came to watch him. He listened to them, arguing with one another, speaking words of love, lamenting, confiding and dreaming out loud as they stood in line, while he waited behind a curtain to entertain them with his tricks of writing with his feet and playing silly little tunes on the special keyboard. When the curtain was drawn and the people who had waited in line, passing the time in talk got quiet and watched him, he watched them back and tried to put the faces together with what he had heard, not just the voices but the stories. Who looked like she was in love with her sister's husband? Who looked like he was still angry at his wife by his side? Ah, that child with the tear-stained face must have been the one nagging his parents for a bicycle, the one who couldn't get quiet, so got spanked instead. A mother told her three-year-old daughter she could cry all she wanted...but James couldn't hear the rest. He noticed that the child was barefoot and wearing only a sleeveless shirt and the mother wore a jacket in the pre-storm wind, and he said right out loud, calling to her in the crowd in a loud voice, "Can't you see, she's cold. Give her your jacket, poor baby," said James not much bigger, but older, much older, and the woman gave him an evil look and walked away to complain to someone about the freak who was supposed to do tricks and talked to the audience instead.

By the time James was seven, Tatum had the idea of letting him make an act of it, pretend to be a psychic and take money to tell folks about their lives and make some vague predictions about the future. James was good at this and always tried to give a little good advice as well, so he wouldn't feel so bad about conning the people. He never forgot a face, and if he eavesdropped on some conversation and then tied a face to the talk, he could place that same person the next year and the next, season after season, as they returned to the same towns year after year. He might have made friends of these country people, so easy to please and impress, but he was a freak, so they never really looked into his eyes, too embarrassed that they had looked at him with curiosity, maybe even horror. So they never recognized him as the same armless child they had seen the year before, even though they must have realized, had they thought about it, that there couldn't be that many like him or he wouldn't be worth paying money to see.

But such philosophical observations made James laugh, not bitter, and he was the comfort of the Carnival della Strega. The carnival was a world unto itself, and there were marriages and separations and affairs going on all the time among that tight little group, and sooner or later all of them had occasion to go see James and confide in him, ask him what to say to whom, and when, and how, and he would try to guide them in the ways of kindness and listen patiently when they came back to tell him what new trouble they'd gotten into ignoring his advice the last time, and soon he learned just to listen and sympathize, because people did whatever they were going to do anyway. At such times he was usually asked to dispense his forgiveness, which he did, puzzled as to why all these people thought they needed it. The Italian family, whose name was not Strega, which means witch, but Bevilaqua, which means drinkwater, and is not the kind of glamorous or interesting name suitable for a traveling carnival, came to see James most often, either in a group or in couples or individually. There were the father and mother, the mother being the only one in the family who didn't perform on the highwire, being easily three hundred pounds, and five daughters and the husbands of four of the daughters, the youngest daughter, being only twelve and too young to marry herself, and all of them harbored resentments against each other most all the time, and James had his hands full, so to speak, keeping them calmed down enough to perform. For this alone, Tatum told him he was worth his keep.

The daughters were all richly gorgeous with thick black hair that curled down their shapely backs and long black lashes that curled on their round, red cheeks, and full lips and huge luminous eyes. One of the middle daughters was married to the handsomest of the sons-in-law, but he was also hot tempered and beat her occasionally, whereupon the father would beat him, even though he was a smaller man, but he had his anger of course, and murderous it was, so the son-in-law would leave and then catch up with the carnival in the next town, get drunk with his father-in-law and make up with his wife and the whole cycle would start all over again. The middle daughter was becoming more and more unhappy and less and less in love with her magnificent husband. She told James then that it was too bad he didn't have arms, because if he did, he would have lots of women in love with him, his kind voice and sweet, deep eyes, and she hugged him and kissed him, and he longed for arms to hug her back. "Why don't you leave him?" he asked her, and she said she had nowhere to go and anyway they all owed Tatum too much money to leave. James was ten then and learned for the first time that he and his mother, like most of the folks in the carnival were virtual slaves to Tatum, who claimed that they owed him so much money and everyone was working off a debt that increased daily. He kept the records, and the records always favored him. Tatum paid all the bills, the grocer, the tailor, the cobbler, the doctor, the lawyer, the judge, the bailbondsman, the blacksmith, the veterinarian, the wheelwright, but Tatum never paid his people, and well he didn't, for if he did, as he was only too glad to point out, their money would be thrown away on the wind and they'd be in even greater debt to their benefactor, as he truly considered himself to be.

This slavery was perhaps not too terrible, as those that did leave the carnival, to marry or maybe because they needed medical care somewhere along the way for an injury or illness and some that served a jail term that Tatum couldn't wait on, those that did leave the carnival for whatever reason always felt as though they'd fallen off a fast moving train and they'd just live out their lives waiting for Tatum to come through again and pick them up so they could resume their old lives where they'd left off. No one ever seemed to get used to not being in the carnival. It wasn't the excitement so much as the fact that folks didn't have to stay any place too long, moving around like they did, they started to feeling forever young, like getting old could only happen if you stayed put long enough for age to catch up with you.

Poor Señora Bevilaqua had to be left behind when her heart got so weak that she frightened them every other night with attacks she knew would be the death of her. Some thought she was trying to get attention from her husband, who was fooling around with a girl his daughter's age, but she didn't get it. It was Tatum who showed her uncharacteristic kindness and the rumor was he'd been in love with her a long time and a couple hundred pounds ago when she was a performer herself, but she chose to marry Bevilaqua and they started the show, and then Tatum showed up in their lives and won the Carnival della Strega in a wager that it was further rumored he'd rigged, all this of course, to get revenge for his broken heart. James had heard the story from several of the carnival folks, and it did seem to him that Tatum did show her a tender respect. In fact after they left her in a town not far from Huntington in Lincoln County, West Virginia, it was Tatum who seemed to truly miss her. She took up with a trucker there she met when selling eggs at a roadside stand, and they bought a little house with a cow and some chickens, and she said she was happier being settled and once a year Tatum would visit her and make some excuse why her fickle little husband didn't, but of course she knew and she regretted the wrong choice she had made a quarter century earlier, which was perhaps just the revenge Tatum wanted after all. Tatum himself had a club foot and suspected that was the reason the señora had preferred the handsome Bevilaqua, whose only impairment was his mind. Of course, to her face, Tatum was the soul of kindness and certainly by then he could afford to be.

"Ah, romance," intoned James melodramatically to his mother as he recited the gossip of the day. But when James told it, it was beyond gossip and became a wise and true running commentary on human nature, as it played itself out in their insulated little world. Neither James nor Mary would have known where to go had they the choice. No, they would have set themselves down somewhere, a drugstore, maybe, nursing sodas and watched out the window waiting for Tatum to come get them.

Mary had told James many times about his birth and about John Banks, and James got to wondering if John Banks had gotten much money for them. Mary was appalled at the idea, but James said he saw it happen all the time and he figured that Mr. Banks must have gotten something and it seemed a point of pride with James that he thought Tatum had paid a goodly sum for the two of them. He wanted to ask and once even did, but Tatum told him to stop being cute, and that was the end of it.

During the winter months Tatum took the entire crew down south, booking a few performances in Gulf Coast towns, but mostly finding old friends that would help the group survive the winter. Missing her garden while on the road, Mary learned to love the wild lands of the Florida Everglades and the Louisiana Bayou country, and the sounds of large birds squawking above her made her dream of jungles in even further lands. Tatum knew that neither Mary nor James was inclined to run away, or get drunk, or fight, or otherwise get themselves into trouble with the local law, so he allowed them unlimited freedom to explore. What Mary and James liked to do with their limited funds, was ride the streetcars. They'd get on the first one to arrive at their stop, ride it to the end of the line and then take another. They would eavesdrop on the conversations of other passengers and sometimes when they were doing a show, would recognize some of the customers from their streetcar reconnoitering. Usually by dusk, they'd be hopelessly lost and have to find their way back by asking the drivers for directions or even for rides. It happened more than once that a driver, finished with his shift would drive them back to the carnival on his way home from work. Sometimes drivers took them home to dinner and sometimes they stayed with the carnival folks for dinner and in this way, Mary and James made a few friends and drew even larger crowds to the shows. Such far-ranging exploration would have terrified Mary had not James reassured her, and so once again it was the child's inventiveness and curiosity that benefitted his employer, and Tatum decided to send other members of the troupe out into the towns to drum up audiences, but no one was quite as successful as James

Sanchez

leading his timid young mother through the land.

Despite her need for the green of trees and gardens, Mary also was fascinated by the vast expanse of water and the broad sandy beaches along the gulf. All by herself she talked Tatum into doing a show on the beach in Biloxi, and they got permission and camped on the beach and set up the tents, the cages, the carousel, and waited for the folks who came in dribs and drabs and then finally droves, and every year they returned to the beach in Mississippi, where James could lie on the beach and watch the shrimping boats drift by and let his lungs clear up, for every year James got bronchial infections and sometimes a mild pneumonia when the leaves fell in the mountains back home.

Each year they had Christmas in a different place, until the Christmas they spent with a woman in Virginia Beach. She was a painter and believed in the prophecies of Edgar Cayce. Tatum fell in love with her and pretended to be interested in the prophecies and admired her paintings, sincerely in fact. James was eleven when they started spending every Christmas in Virginia Beach, and Mary didn't mind, even though she missed the traditional setting in the snowy Appalachians because the woman, who had taken the name Dorothea to dress up her given name of Dorothy, was delighted with James. He had already displayed the perception that made folks believe he was psychic, and Dorothea was certain that he was a modern day prophet just like Edgar Cayce. She painted James in many forms and backgrounds, sometimes with the wings of an eagle or the arms of a bear, surrounded by the forest and the sky, and she told Mary that God had marked James in that special way to be an example of the beauty of a gentle spirit to all around him. "After all, when you think about it, what do men use their arms for? For acts of violence and even that word 'arms' means not only human limbs but also human weaponry designed to make war, so you see there was a message in James's birth." Mary was astounded and said without thinking that she'd wished John Banks would have thought of that, and when Dorothea asked her about John Banks, Mary had no choice but to simply tell her the story, even though it embarrassed her to admit her part in the great con, as some folks had called it. "Why a con? Haven't I just told you that James is special? Maybe he is the Christ come back to earth to offer comfort and see what progress his flock has made. Why does that shock you? well, if you feel sacrilegious even thinking that, then might I suggest that you take seriously my intuition that James is a prophet with an important purpose here on earth?" So that was a very special Christmas for Mary. And each Christmas thereafter as well, for each year Dorothea presented her with a portrait of James, a small copy of the larger canvas that she would sell to visitors who came to her gallery in her home from as far away as New York City and even California; people who came to study at the Association for Research and Enlightenment and were directed to her studio because she was known as a woman of vision.

It was Dorothea who predicted Pearl Harbor, based on her readings of Cayce's journals and, unfortunately, it was Dorothea who predicted James's death on the eve of that horrendous event.

"You're just saying that because he's so sick, but he gets like this every year and he always gets better."

"It isn't the pneumonia, Mary, it's a dream that I had about James, but in my dream he wasn't James, he was someone else, and I knew that he was also James. Do you believe in reincarnation, Mary?"

"I don't even know what that is. Is that something you read about over there?"

"Yes, Edgar Cayce talked about reincarnation but he hasn't been the only one. I have always known about it. Other religions believe in it and Christians have argued about it. Have you ever heard of Nicodemas? He made predictions about our world just like Cayce has. And he taught reincarnation also. It is simple really, You already believe that the soul doesn't die don't you?"

"I guess, I don't really know. I'm not sure I know what the soul is."

"Oh Mary, none of us knows for sure, but we feel it, and why should the soul be gone just because our bodies die and decay? Think of it like water, Mary. When water freezes it becomes ice, but when ice melts it doesn't disappear, it becomes water, and when water gets very hot and turns to steam, it doesn't disappear, it becomes steam or clouds and steam becomes water again and clouds rain. Why can't the soul have that kind of eternal existence, taking different forms?"

"No reason I guess, but why are you telling me this? Are you saying I shouldn't grieve if James dies because his soul will come back? Will I recognize him? You know I can't live without my son. He is all I have."

And Mary got very quiet, not able to bear the thought of James dying, not wanting to believe Dorothea, but afraid that Dorothea would say something that would make her have to believe her. She was curious to hear Dorothea's dream, but afraid as well. And Dorothea, afraid she was losing Mary, pressed on, gently, like talking to a child about death, because Mary seemed like a child to her, even though Mary lied about her age to everyone including Dorothea, because she didn't want anyone to know that James had been born when she was only 13. Dorothea took her hand, her tiny, childlike hand, and told her about her dream.

It was a quiet uneventful dream really, but it startled Mary. Dorothea dreamed she stood by the entrance of a cave with a woman who had long black hair that hung to her knees and the woman was dark skinned, Dorothea thought she was Indian and told Mary that she had always felt a rapport with Indians and their lifestyle. The woman was trying to coax Dorothea into the cave and Dorothea was afraid, but the woman finally convinced her that she would be safe, and they went together into a room at the mouth of the cave where a fire burned, and there were animals lying about the fire.

They were animals that in real life would have frightened her, but in the dream, Dorothea was not afraid of the mountain lion, the bear or the snake. Then the man came in after them, the man who was older and larger than James, but who Dorothea somehow knew was or would be James, and he told the two women that he had come to the cave to find out what to do, for he was about to die and knew he needed to come back in another form and make amends for mistakes he had made in this life. So the woman spoke to him in a kind of rhyme, which Dorothea tried to remember when she awoke, but she couldn't remember the rhyme. It had something to do with his arms, and that was how she knew he would come back as James, with no arms, for he had used his arms to do an evil thing and he was sorry and he would pay by being reborn with no arms at all.

Dorothea knew nothing of Mary's childhood and couldn't have known how the story of her dream would affect the guilt-stricken woman. "It's all my fault then," was all Mary would say and then she left, late as it was, dark as it was and walked the beach to cry and tear her hair, for she was sure that James bore the punishment for her sin and she thought of all the warnings she should have heeded. If only the preacher had talked to her, warned her that if she didn't do penance for her deeds, her child would. And now she had no doubt that James would die and leave her alone to dwell forever in her guilt and despair. Mary was hysterical and ran into the ocean thinking to die there, but as soon as the waves knocked her down, her body began to fight and she gasped for air and struggled to stay above the thick and angry night waters, and then she felt arms reaching for her and it was Dorothea herself who pulled her out of the ocean, and as they lay on the hard packed sand, Mary cried and lamented, "I don't even know how to drown, what will I do? I can't even die." And Dorothea comforted her like a mother until Mary, exhausted, slept.

They slept on the beach until the dawn woke them and Mary got up with a sick feeling that James had died in the night without her and she couldn't run fast enough to the house where he lay sick and dying, but still conscious, and Mary was so relieved to be able to say good-bye to him that his death was not the shock it might have been. It was coming on Christmas and Mary promised her son that this Christmas he was in pain but next Christmas would be better, for their Christmases together had always been very special. And James understood her and held her in his deep, sweet brown eyes, fathomless eyes, and Mary drowned her grief and guilt in those eyes, for surely no one had lived such a loving life as her son James, and she listened eagerly thereafter to all the comforting thoughts that Dorothea spoke to her, and she did live.

Tatum paid the funeral expenses and there was a large turnout and the orchestra played beautiful, stately, sad music, and then it was over, her son interred and buried beneath the sand and gravel and dirt in an oceanside cemetery. Dorothea promised to keep it well planted, as Mary would be gone during the spring and summer months. Neither woman knew then that Mary would never come back to her son's grave.

XIII

After James died, Tatum told Mary she was free to go, as if he was doing her a favor, but even Mary could see it was because she was useless to him now James was gone. She told him she had nowhere to go, a fact he was well aware of, and begged him to let her stay a while so she could look for work. What work he wondered, and she came up with the idea of housekeeper, because all she knew how to do was take care of a child and cook and clean up. Well that and the sewing she'd done for the performers sometimes…she could sew too. But Mary had no idea where to go looking for work and in the end it was Tatum himself who found her a position, because he knew even he couldn't put her out on the street with nowhere to go, and her just a child when she'd come to him in the first place.

Roger Adkins had married himself a city girl and when it come time for him to go off to war, she didn't want to stay on the farm with his mother and sisters, but insisted she'd go back to Covington and live with her own mother until he was back home, and she thought she'd like to get herself a job because she read where some factories were hiring women now with the men all off to war. So she was wanting a girl to stay with them; to look after her son and her mother, who was old now and sickly, while she was away at her job. They couldn't afford to pay Mary a wage, but she'd have a roof over her head and three meals a day and be doing what she'd always done. Mary was happy to be caring for a little boy again, different as he was from her own sweet James. So Mary went to live in the city until the war was over and she stayed pretty much to the house and the garden, as her employer always brought the groceries home with her when she came in from work, and Mary was fine with that, being afraid of the city anyway.

Roxy, short for Roxanne, was bold like the carnival women, and Mary was used to that, so they got along real well until Roxy noticed she was doing all the talking and that she didn't really know a thing about the woman who lived under their roof and cared for her son. But Mary couldn't be brought out in conversation, answering specific questions simply and directly and offering nothing further, no train of thought to follow to one subject after another the way Roxy was used to with her friends at the factory, all of them high on the new freedom and financial independence they felt, having so many things in common: men off to war and the worry of it and the children growing up so fast, ailing parents, times a changing, the weather if all else failed them in their brief moments of camaraderie at break time and after work walking to the streetcar. They all had sisters, or aunts, or grandparents at home looking after the children, and Roxy never did tell anyone that Mary wasn't a relative, not wanting to he others to think she was too high and mighty, having her a housekeeper, a stranger to do the chores at home. There'd come a time soon enough, after the war, when the family moved to Denver to follow an opportunity that proved profitable, when Roxy would insist that folks use her full name and she'd hold her nose in the air with the best of them. Then she'd treat Mary with more distance, more authority, but for now she just wanted to get to know her and resented it slightly that Mary didn't seem to reciprocate her friendliness.

Mary was good with little Roger, though, taking him with her into the garden and teaching him the plants, teaching him some songs she knew. Roger loved her and she loved him. Sometimes they danced to music on the radio, but that was their secret, for Roger's mother would not approve of a little boy like that dancing like a girl, or so she'd think, because that's what Roger's father would think. Roxy herself liked to talk tough like a man and didn't care for women who were "prissy." Mary was afraid if she talked too much to Roxy, her employer would think her prissy in spite of her interesting life with the carnival. Roxy always asked Mary questions about the carnival, as if she thought it were all just as much fun for the people who worked in it as it was for the folks who paid their admission to escape their own daily lives of work, work, work and bills to pay and people to argue with about one thing or another.

Mary and little Roger never got caught because the news would come on just about the time Roxy came home and they would sit still and listen like they just lived to hear the nightly news about the war. Roxy joined them and it seemed she really did live to hear the news, like she was expecting to hear about her husband right there on the national news, and she imagined him getting some medal for heroism, but she never imagined him getting killed. If her mind started to work in that direction, she would stop herself with a prayer. Once she did imagine he came home without his legs and she was his loving wife and nurse but when she caught herself feeling righteous at his expense, she stopped and told herself to settle down and pray for his safe return. She saw too many movies and sometimes took them too seriously. No, certainly if she wanted to know what real people did in those kinds of terrible circumstances, she had only to look around her at her own neighbors and listen to their stories. Just up the street was a WWI veteran who had lost his legs, and his wife had left him not long after he came back from France, and he was a mean and bitter human being. She knew when she thought about it that life wasn't going to be

Sanchez

like the movies. She knew when she thought about it that for her, life would never be as good as she dreamed about, but at least it would never be as bad as she sometimes feared. Roxy's problem was she had too much imagination. As a girl people were always telling her how good looking she was and that she should be in the movies, and they said it like it wasn't really her dream, just some nice thing to say, a meaningless compliment because no one they knew really did that. Roxy longed to go out to California and be a movie star and even started saving money for the train, but then Roger came along and she married him, she wasn't sure why now she thought about it, but she did and there she was.

Being a working woman was exciting for Roxy and she enjoyed sharing her excitement with Mary, who listened and smiled and sometimes encouraged her. There were flirtations at work, and then Roxy started coming home later and later and one night not at all, and Mary was afraid to say anything to her about it, but she stopped smiling and listening, and finally Roxy broached the subject herself, asking Mary if she disapproved, as if Mary's opinion was important. Mary didn't know how to react, so she changed the subject and for the first time began telling Roxy a little about herself. "I had a son once myself but he died. He was only 13. Would you like to see a picture of him?" She didn't ever volunteer to show anyone her photos of James, because the first and last time she had done so, the woman had gasped upon seeing that he had no arms, but when she showed Roxy the first photo, Roxy just said he was a cute baby and asked what happened to his arms, as if it were not so uncommon, and Mary explained he had been born that way, and Roxy didn't apologize, just repeated that he was a cute baby, so Mary showed her the rest of the photos, one for each of his thirteen years, and Roxy said it was a shame he died so young and asked what he died of, and Mary explained he'd always been sickly and had chronic bronchial problems and finally got pneumonia so bad it killed him, and Roxy said again what a shame it was, and neither one said anything after that, but just sat a while, and then Roxy told Mary that her lover had dumped her and she'd be coming home to see her and Roger every night and they'd all eat dinner together like they used to, and she'd learned her lesson not to let no fool of a man use her and dump her, and what did she need a man for anyway, with her dear little son waiting for her every night? It took one more fool of a man to teach her good and proper in the fall of the year when the colors of the trees and the brilliance of the skies filled young hearts with passion and a heightened sense of the tragedy of life, but by Christmas, all was well again, which was handy, because Roger senior came home then for a visit, bringing cowboy shirts for everyone and little boy sized chaps for his son and stories about the wild west, where he'd been stationed a while in

118

Denver, Colorado. He was on his way then to England, from where he would fly bombing missions over France, and he was all excited about ending the war once and for all, never dreaming it would be yet another two years before it ended. He promised them all, as if they'd been dreaming of it all their lives, that they were going to move out to Denver when the war was over, that he'd make some friends out there and had a job already lined up selling luggage around the country. Roxy wasn't all that impressed, but he kept talking about an up and coming company and getting in at the ground floor, and later he'd turn out to be right and of course everyone was hyped-up with hope and ambition in those days. Mary thought about the people who came to see her give birth to James, needing to escape from the world they knew and then the revelers at the carnival, still escaping, and now here were all these folks who wanted to jump right into the world and make something of their lives, as if they had the power to do that all by themselves. No one thought about God anymore. Mary didn't know if that was good or bad and of course, no one asked her anyway. Only Roxy sometimes asked her, "Do you believe in God, Mary?"..."Do you think God will forgive me, Mary?"

During the four years that Mary lived with Roxy and Roger in Covington, she hardly spoke at all to Roxy's mother, who was not only sickly, but seemed a little gone in the head. There'd been a companion for her before Roxy came home with Mary and she was sent back to the farm that she'd come from and seemed glad enough to go. She told Mary on her way out that the woman was impossible, never knew what she wanted, but would wear a person out asking. Maybe having her daughter and grandson back home was what she wanted, because she rarely asked Mary for anything. In the winter when it was cold and wet, she'd stay in bed most of the time listening to the radio and eating like a bird from a tray that Mary would bring her. But in the spring, she would want to go out to the garden and plant a few beans and potatoes. She'd been a farm girl herself as were most of the citizens of that town, coming in only to get the jobs at the paper mills when they couldn't make it anymore on the farms. Many of them still owned their land and would leave their jobs at 5 o'clock, only to drive out to the country and harvest their hay in the long summer evenings. Mary would follow the old mother, Hester, her name was, and help her dig and sow and later to weed. Once when Roger pulled up some tiny tomato plants, Mary had to teach him to pinch the little leaves and smell his fingers, so he could tell which were the weeds that smelled generically of the earth and which were the fruits and flowers they desired to cultivate and smelled sweet and desirable. "That's right," said Hester, who smiled at Mary and loved her ever after because she appreciated the scents of the garden. It didn't take much to please an old farm mother. It was Mary who reminded

Roxy when they moved out to Denver after the war that they'd need to find a place with a garden for the old mother. Every winter Hester would fade away almost to death but be reborn and sprightly again come spring, so Mary understood that without the garden, Hester would fade away forever. And Hester confided in Mary that she thought her daughter talked too much, so she didn't have a chance to listen and understand anything, but she didn't care now because she had Mary. Hester herself hardly ever talked but hummed most of the time some music she made up in her head, and when she did that she moved eloquently almost like dancing, but timid and subtle. Roxy called her senile, but Hester didn't care, because she knew Mary understood her and would look after her needs.

By the time they moved to Denver, Roger was old enough to go to school all day every day and Mary's work was mostly to clean the house, which was large and full of the fancy furniture Roxy bought like there was no tomorrow. And she cooked the dinner too, but she didn't eat with the family anymore in the fancy dining room. She had her dinner alone in the kitchen, or in Hester's bedroom when she was invited. Sometimes Hester slept through dinner. When the weather was mild Mary would take Hester on the bus to the City Park, and they would walk slowly around the lake there. Sometimes there were band concerts in the evenings and the whole family would go in the new car that Roger bought for them, a Cadillac, he reminded them and was very proud. But in the winter the days were as long and lonely as the nights until Roger brought home the television set, and then Hester and Mary both would watch in fascination westerns and mysteries and comedies. Every Saturday a man with an English accent introduced different programs of theater, opera and ballet, and Mary saw for the first time the ballet. Maria Tallchief, she would never forget that name, performed a dance from Swan Lake, and Mary wanted to dance like Maria Tallchief. She was already in her mid-thirties but knowing nothing about ballet, she thought she could still learn. She already knew some of the stately movements from watching the carnival performers in their leotards, but of course they had never danced like Maria Tallchief to such exquisite music.

Mary asked Roxy about it and Roxy made some phone calls and told her where she could go to take ballet lessons and how to get there on the bus and when she could take time off to do it. Roxy still didn't pay Mary any wages, but she gave her money for ballet lessons, and Mary took the written directions and told the driver where she had to go so he could tell her when to get off and where to catch the bus to come home again. But all the ballet students were children and already knew more than she did, so Mary never even talked to the teacher about lessons but came home again crying and then Roxy laughed at her, gently enough but Mary was confused. Mary got confused so easily about almost anything, Roxy had noticed but it never occurred to her to teach Mary confidence. Mary blushed deep red and hot whenever she thought of the harsh old woman at the ballet school who had seen her hovering at the door and asked her in a fuzzy, angry sounding accent what she wanted, and all Mary could think of to do was turn and run down the three flights of stairs, crying all the way, crying as she gave the bus driver her fare and crying all the way home in front of all the passengers. She was embarrassed to ride that bus again and would walk several blocks out of her way to avoid it, not just because the driver had seen her cry, but because he knew she had gone to the ballet school and probably knew that only children went there. But Mary still watched. She watched *The Red Shoes* on the television and cried and cried when the dancer threw herself under the train, feeling as if she knew exactly how she felt, for she would like to have danced herself to death if she only could. And when the Ballet Russe de Monte Carlo came to Denver, she got the money and permission to go to the Sunday matinee. The ballet teacher was there and so were many of the little girls, but Mary hid and hoped they didn't see her. Mary looked for Maria Tallchief's name in the program, but she didn't see it. Ruthana Boris was the leading ballerina and she was lovely, but Mary would always prefer Maria Tallchief, because she was the first.

Mary wanted to dance in the basement of the house where there was room to move across the floor, but the only time she had the house to herself was when she skipped church, so now she stopped going to church altogether, which worried Roxy, who thought that Mary was growing sick and depressed, but Mary insisted she was alright and said she liked to pray alone and indeed her dancing was like a prayer, for she put into it all of her hope and all of her joy. She imitated the steps she saw on TV and the steps she saw at the auditorium when the Ballet Ruse came to Denver to perform, and she made up some movements of her own to the music on the record player. She had asked Roxy to buy her records of Liszt and Chopin and Tchaikovsky, names she saw in the ballet programs, and Roxy was impressed and tried to tease her, but Mary became so red and confused that even Roxy had to pay attention and stop. Mary would dance until she heard the family come back from church, and then she would run over to the sofa in the corner and sit very still, pretending to be listening to the music, quietly. Once little Roger thought he knew what she was up to and asked "Dancing again, Mary?" and she just glared at him in a way she had never done before, not an angry glare but a look of desperate fear that puzzled him.

Big Roger, as they called him, put a basketball hoop up on the side of the garage, and he and little Roger played basketball on the driveway in the summer evenings after work and school and on the weekends. Mary watched from her window in the house and missed James, and sometimes she dreamed of her son grown with arms that he wrapped around her. Sometimes she dreamed of her father and woke up in a sweat, with her heart beating too hard and too fast.

They meant well but just didn't understand, like Hester always said: Roxy and her husband and son all talked too much and didn't really listen or pay attention. What they did was spy on her, making her think they'd left for church and then coming down as quiet as mice after the music began playing, watching silently while she danced until the music ended and they all applauded like she was some ballet dancer on the stage and shouting bravo Mary. What could have possessed them to think that a 39-year-old woman would be proud to perform for them? Mary was deeply mortified and was too shocked to even cry or blush, but retired to her room with as much dignity as she had in her and remained there until Hester herself hobbled down to ask her to come out and eat dinner. Mary resumed her chores around the house without a word to anyone and continued silent for weeks. None of them could find the words to apologize to Mary, for none of them truly understood the depth of the offense, so they continued in silence until Hester talked her out of her humiliation, and they all tried to act as if nothing had happened and soon things settled back to normal for the family, except, of course, for Mary, who never danced again, but once.

When little Roger, who by now towered over his father, packed an old car to drive up to Boulder for college, Mary stayed in her room and wouldn't help. She heard Roxy tell Roger to go find her and say good-bye and Roger tell his mother that he didn't think Mary cared for him anymore, and it irritated her that they didn't even whisper, knowing she could hear everything that went on in that driveway, but then when he did come down and looked at her with eyes full of love and chagrin, she forgave him for not being her son, and hugged him long and hard and cried, thinking of her James, who never grew up. "It isn't that far, Mary, and I'll be coming home on weekends," he told her, thinking that her tears were all for him.

Roger was busy with a fraternity and parties and friends and did not in fact come home on weekends until the weekend of his grandmother's funeral. Hester finally died at the age of 90, even though she had been happily pruning and mulching her rosebushes for the winter that very morning. She had once told Mary that as long as she had a garden, she would live, forever maybe, that gardening was the key to long life, and Mary had wondered why Hester told her that, because Mary didn't really want a long life, not since her child had died. Life had been a slow business for Mary even before that, ever since her moment of ruined glory on the mountaintop in West Virginia, when James was born and she'd been abandoned first by all the zealous followers and then by John Banks himself, who had saved her life and for what, she often wondered. But lately things had started speeding up again with little Roger leaving home and then Hester dying. She hadn't expected it, but something made her tell Hester just the night before, that her real name was Mary Queen of Scots, because she wanted someone to know her full name, and Hester had responded that her full name was Hester Elizabeth, but she didn't expect anyone would remember that until her funeral. And then, there it was, Hester Elizabeth's funeral, and indeed they did remember, and the name was carved in all its lengthy glory on the tombstone, over the dates 1868 to 1958.

Mary missed Hester, but even more than missing her, she envied her, for she dreaded a long sojourn in other people's lives. She had been with little Roger longer than she had been with her own son, and yet she didn't feel like she belonged, sleeping in the basement, eating in the kitchen. She began to pray every night that God would take her in her sleep, peacefully and painlessly like he had taken Hester, but then she would dream of dying violent deaths, usually by drowning, sometimes being buried alive, and then she would throw off the covers and gasp for air, afraid to fall back asleep. She would get out of bed before dawn and go walking in the park, and Roxy would warn her not to do that, there were drunks in the park, she could be raped, Roxy said. But Mary, sick of life and wanting to die, felt invincible and continued her dawn walks to calm her soul and soothe her pounding heart after her nights of terror.

On a crisp morning in April, when snow still glistened on the grass and flowers that had sprung forth during the warm weeks of March and the distant peaks were blue and white, Mary heard the birds, and they sounded like summer to her. She always paid attention to the birds now, as they heralded the seasons and woke her in the mornings with news of sun or storm, and it seemed to Mary that a sleek magpie that hopped down on the grass near her, anticipating bread crumbs, looked straight at her and talked to her, and she tried to understand what the bird was telling her. As the sun melted the remains of the last snowstorm and the day grew sweet and warm, the park filled with people, and some men in colorful, flowing shirts played drums and flutes and some women, dressed in leotards and long skirts, danced on the grass in the sun to the music, and they must have noticed the longing in Mary's face, because one woman stopped and approached Mary and invited her to join them, but they were so young and seemed so strange to Mary that she just shook her head and went away. But she decided that the bird must have been telling her that it was okay to dance, and certainly her arms and legs seemed about to move whether she willed it or not. Mary walked fast, nearly ran home and realized that it must be Sunday, because Roxy and Roger were gone, to church it must have been, and Mary locked all the doors and even barricaded them with chairs, and then she put on her favorite recording that played the music of *Swan Lake* and she began to dance all over the house. She imagined that James danced with her, that he had arms and he encircled her with his arms, his arms laying lightly on her arms, so that when she opened her arms, she opened his as well, and when she closed her arms around herself, his arms held her close. His hands gracefully curved around hers and together they reached as high as they could and together they whirled their arms around, forcing their bodies to follow in a dizzying twirl to the ground and up again to reach, the way she had seen on the television. Mary could feel her shoulders begin to move her arms with a strength that felt beautiful, and then each muscle down to her hands that curved to sculpt the air, that turned to wind around her as she moved faster and faster until she fluttered as the music fluttered, slowing to a graceful stop and then moving again, and all the while she could feel her son's arms lie upon her own in the endless dance that was delicate and fluid as a breeze. When the record ended, Mary heard the music in her head and danced and danced until she twirled one last time into a heap on the floor and stayed there quietly humming, or so it seemed to Mary.

When the family was finally able to break into the house, they found Mary dead on the rec room floor, huddled in a ball, her arms wrapped around herself. The doctor speculated that she'd died of an aneurism, a blood vessel burst in her brain. But of course it was too much joy killed Mary Queen of Scots. All that dancing had filled her with more joy than a body could bear.

author's note

Sandra Shwayder Sanchez, an attorney, teacher, and political activist, has a special love for music, nature and literature. Constantly in search for clues to human motivation, past lives and life meanings, her writing is informed by fairy tales, universal mythology, art and music. **Stillbird** *is her second published novel. Ms. Shwayder-Sanchez has also published several articles and short stories. She earned a B.A in Behaviorial Science at University of Maryland and a JD from The University of Denver Law School. In the early seventies she built a house and farmed in rural West Virginia. She lives in Colorado with her husband John Edward Sanchez.*

Forthcoming from The Wessex Collective:

R. P. Burnham

On a Darkling Plain

Samuel Jellerson, 56 and forced into early retirement, is walking in the woods behind the family farm in Maine one fall day when he witnesses a priest molesting a boy. From this one event all the action in the novel follows and draws a wide cross section of the town—a frantic mother, an idealistic teenage girl, a brooding, alienated young man, a priest, a minister, a swamp yankee, a lonely old man, a happy-go-lucky plumber, and many others— into a theme that explores the nature of evil and its antidote empathy, the force that creates community, fellow-feeling and a sense of responsibility to others.

William Davey

The Angry Dust

This exquisite novel tells the story of Prescott Barnes and his family leaving the dust bowl for golden California, but there its similarities with *The Grapes of Wrath* end. The grandson of a wealthy preacher who disinherited Prescott's father, Barnes, despite his cynical black humor, unwavering hostility to religion, and his illiteracy, possesses a fierce integrity and passions that make him larger than life at the same time he is perfectly human. Told with perfect command and in a brilliant style, this is a novel of tragic grandeur in the fine high style of old with the action inevitably leading to tragedy, and tragedy totally flowing from character. In Prescott's case, it is his poverty and hostility toward religion that leads to his tragic mistake. Every character, even the minor ones like Rev. Eberstadt (a con man who nevertheless grows in sincerity and in capacity to love) are revealed in such detail that we get to know them like old friends. The plot unfolds as inevitably as an eclipse, and the forces of nature, like the tornado that strikes them, are vividly and unforgettably described. Most importantly, Prescott Barnes's tragic confrontation with the world compellingly reveals how common people can possess power and grandeur.

Brian E. Backstrand

Little Bluestem: Stories from Rural America

Little bluestem is a vigorous, drought-resistant native bunchgrass. It is well known in the Great Plains and in other places in America's heartland where it frequently is found with other prairie grasses. Most of the people in Brian E. Backstrand's first collection of stories, *Little Bluestem*, would know this hardy plant by sight. They would see it surviving in the ditches and volunteering on the hard-scrabble places of the rural landscapes in which they live. They would understand it to be an ordinary grass which persists and endures.

Backstrand's stories from rural America chronicle often small but important moments of the lives of ordinary people from the farms and the small towns of middle America.   He writes of the man at the local café telling stories for the benefit of some friends while hiding his own struggle with cancer, or the young soldier, home from the war, who at last decides to trust someone with some of the burden of his memories when unexpectedly visited in the midst of a snowstorm by his elderly, compassionate priest.   In another story, a middle-aged woman, about to be wed, discovers that her work as a collector brings her face to face with the humanity of an elderly woman whom she is trained to see simply as another debtor.   In "Side De-livery," an 'old school' farmer, home from an auction, suddenly encounters grief, while in "October Night," a storm on an autumn evening brings tragic illness to a farm couple on an isolated farmstead.

Memories—healing or disruptive, constant or denied—often play an important role in the stories of *Little Bluestem* which link together rural people from vari-ous generations, caught in the midst of struggle or in a moment of recognition or healing. Backstrand's intention is to lift up ordinary people from rural contexts and place them squarely before his contemporary and often urban readers. His stories come as an invitation, asking his readers to consider once more their rural counter-parts who, like the common, native bluestem grass, often are overlooked.

Other books currently available from...

The Wessex Collective

R. P. Burnham   **Envious Shadows**   **228 pages**   **$11.50**

In *Envious Shadows*, R. P. Burnham has given us a full blooded novel, driven by plot, character and issues of racism, sexism, infidelity, the struggle to survive economically in a small Maine town, and the overarching love that can redeem us from sorrow and loss. This is a book that will provoke thought, feeling and rage at hatred and inequity. Surely this is the most we can ask of any writer when we pick up his book.
        –Laurel Speer, poet and former columnist for Small Press Review

Envious Shadows is a marvelous book. It is about a black and white relationship which has strength to resist the intermittent brutality of human nature. The book never lags for a instant, and it is full of realistic details which range from dealing with the psychological integration of half-way house residents into society, the intricacies of the game of softball, the atmosphere of pubs, the challenges facing building contractors, the mindset of the KKK, to the correct planting of roses. There isn't a pompous moment in it and it is loaded with quiet wit, with seriousness, with irony, and through it all there shines not only a knowledge of literature but a knowledge of life.
        –Susan Davey, editor and literary agent

Ita Willen   **The Gift**   **106 pages**   **$9.50**

The close of the Nazi death camps was a beginning rather than an end for those who survived. Told through the eyes of a child of Holocaust survivors, *The Gift* lets us feel the pain and the courage that reaches into the decades beyond the war. Compelling and insightful. A memorable read.
        –Barb Lundy, poet

Every time I read this memoir (and I have read it several times) I am awed by its beauty and insight. Every time I read this memoir I increase my own insights about how I can live my own life more fully.
        –Sandra Shwayder Sanchez, author of *Stillbird* and *The Nun*.

For further information (and forthcoming books) write to The Wessex Collective/1955 Holly/Denver CO 80220, or visit http://www.wessexcollective.com on the web. The books are available from select bookstores or direct. For mail orders please include $2.00 for first book and 50¢ for each additional book for shipping and handling. Checks only, please.